A Novel

VAIKHARI

The Divine Voice

Ragini Prasad

Publisher

NEW LIFE MEDIA

Vaikhari - The Divine Voice (Novel)
Language: English
First Edition: 2025

ISBN: 9788198586223

Disclaimer

This is a work of fiction. Names, characters, places, incidents, and events are either the product of the author's imagination or used fictitiously for narrative purposes. Any resemblance to actual persons, living or dead, or to actual events or places is purely coincidental.
The novel may contain references to cultural, spiritual, or traditional concepts. These are intended solely to serve the story and are not presented as factual or authoritative interpretations.

The publisher and author disclaim any liability arising in connection with the use or interpretation of the content in this book. This work is meant for general reading and literary engagement.

Cover, Layout, Formatting:

New Life Media Enterprises,

Publisher:

New Life Media Enterprises,

Suratgarh (Rajasthan) 335804

Email: newlifemedia101@gmail.com

Web: www.newlifemedia.co.in

Publisher's Note

We are delighted to present ''Vaikhari - The Divine Voice', the English translation of Ragini Prasad's acclaimed Hindi novel ''Vaikhari'. A prolific writer, Ragini Prasad has also authored a poetry collection, a compilation of short stories, another novel, and the original Hindi edition of this powerful work.

In this novel, the author turns a discerning eye toward the persistent gender imbalance in the political domain. With sensitivity and sharp insight, she brings to light the enduring struggles of women in a society that, even after decades of independence, continues to deny them equal standing.

Despite legal reforms and the establishment of institutions like Women's Commissions, women are still largely confined to secondary roles—both in family structures and public life. Their identities are too often defined by their relationships, especially within marriage, while entrenched patriarchal attitudes continue to favour men and boys. This systemic bias breeds both subtle and overt forms of exploitation.

One of the most striking examples explored in the novel is the denial of daughters' rightful claim to inheritance. Though the law permits equal rights, many women are silenced by emotional pressure, social expectations, and deep-rooted traditions that favour sons. Fathers routinely pass on their property to sons, sidelining daughters, who often accept this injustice without protest.

Only a few women manage to overcome significant obstacles to build independent identities, frequently contending with opposition from structures that should empower them. Nowhere is this imbalance more apparent than in politics, where women remain vastly underrepresented and struggle to be heard within a system that resists meaningful inclusivity. Even those who rise to positions of power often find themselves constrained by party politics and male-dominated agendas.

The fact that India has not seen a woman Prime Minister since Indira Gandhi stands as a stark reminder of this continuing exclusion. This novel holds up a mirror to these uncomfortable truths, using fiction as a tool to provoke thought and inspire dialogue.

With a gripping narrative and deep social relevance, Ragini Prasad urges us to reconsider our definitions of power, representation, and justice. Her storytelling not only reflects the lived realities of countless women but also underscores the urgent need for systemic change.

We look forward to your reflections on this significant work.

Omesh Verma,
(Publisher)
Email: writersdunia@gmail.com

Preface

Ragini Prasad, a lawyer by profession and a literary enthusiast since childhood, is now reaching a pivotal moment in her literary career. This work should be understood through the lens of Ragini Prasad's intellectual depth and insightful perspective.

As a lawyer, she possesses a discerning awareness of the intricate dynamics of political, social, and personal realms. Prasad's multifaceted personality is imbued with a maturity that stems from her dedication to advocating for women's legal rights. In her thoughtful reflections, she emphasizes the plight of educated women who, despite their ambitions, often find themselves victims of oppression. Throughout her legal battles for women's rights, she has discerned the internal complexities that women face. She articulates that women's psychology differs from that of men; they often struggle to suppress their innate compassion.

Regrettably, even with constitutional guarantees, women still grapple with inequality—a profound irony that Ragini Prasad captures with remarkable subtlety. Her novel “Vaikhari - The Divine Voice” serves as a powerful conduit for her expansive experiences and insights, effectively awakening spiritual consciousness within its narrative. It transcends scholarly discourse, presenting a captivating interplay of intellect and emotion on a broad canvas. The overarching themes continually remind readers of the relentless challenges women encounter throughout their lives.

At the heart of “Vaikhari - The Divine Voice” lies the exploration of the journey from political engagement to moral and spiritual dilemmas, encapsulating both resolved and unresolved issues.

The novel’s protagonist, Amrita, aspires to pursue education, viewing it as a crucial tool for women's empowerment. She and her mother believe that education can forge new pathways for women, from rural origins to urban opportunities, and from ignorance to enlightenment. Through education, Amrita ascends in the political realm, often reflecting on her parents' guidance during turbulent times. Ragini Prasad's keen political awareness and life philosophy enhance the narrative.

Amrita's love marriage to Amit challenges societal norms, prompting questions about whether such a union is a revolutionary act or a misguided choice—debates often dictated by societal judgments. The novel conveys an undercurrent of rebellion while also pondering why marital bonds can lead to friction between once-close companions. It underscores the societal lens through which women's experiences are viewed, often leaving them vulnerable to judgment. Ragini Prasad authentically captures Amrita as a fully realized character, complete with aspirations and desires.

Amrita's political journey is portrayed as a significant milestone, challenging societal expectations of women. The narrative probes whether politics is a treacherous domain where women risk losing their identity and dignity, or if it becomes a consuming obsession that complicates their existence. The struggle of being a politician, wife, and mother weighs upon Amrita, whose family often fails to comprehend her multifaceted roles, burdening her with expectations. Despite the multitude of conflicts and struggles she faces, the author's portrayal of Amrita's resilience and will to persevere is compelling.

The essence of "Vaikhari - The Divine Voice" resonates deeply throughout the narrative, particularly as Amrita seeks solace in spiritual reflections amid her many trials. She recalls the tranquillity and wisdom found in the ashram, where she experiences profound introspection that touches her soul.

In "Vaikhari - The Divine Voice", Ragini Prasad artfully articulates the mantra for achieving success through deliberate action and spiritual fulfilment. The novel instills a sense of inquiry, urging readers to consider the unseen forces behind a woman’s triumphs. Who are the political figures who exploit women and reduce them to mere objects of desire? What societal forces seek to suppress women through coercion? What aspirations and emotional entanglements hinder their personal journeys? Prasad's writing lays bare the vulnerabilities of humanity without resorting to superficial ideals, engaging readers with authentic explorations of ambition and relationship dynamics.

Manju Chaturvedi,
Senior Litterateur,
Udaipur, Rajastthan.

AUTHOR'S WORD

"Vaikhari - The Divine Voice" is a novel that explores the role of women in the realm of politics. Through the character of its protagonist, this realistic narrative examines the complexities of a woman's life as a politician, mother, wife, and daughter. This story highlights the modern political scene and looks into the emotional challenges faced by a woman who steps beyond tradition, showing how she handles the tough world of ambition, power plays, and strategies involving women's reservation rights.

The protagonist's inner conflict becomes a source of empowerment; while men in politics face their own struggles, those differ significantly from the challenges faced by women. The heroine is acutely aware of the conspiracies surrounding her and possesses the wisdom to navigate them. By thwarting the schemes of self-serving men, she adeptly manages all the situations deliberately orchestrated against her. This character is crafted to embody a deep awareness of her existence, continually reflecting on her purpose in life amidst the labyrinth of political sub consciousness. She adapts to various circumstances and recognizes that adversity can sometimes be a necessary step toward achievement.

In her ongoing quest for identity—essentially seeking the question, "Who am I?"—the heroine immerses herself in daily responsibilities while pursuing her personal truth. Though her life may appear solitary, her purpose transcends the interests of a few and reaches out to society as a whole.

Throughout her journey from womanhood to a broader humanity, she confidently expresses herself as an individual beyond gender, enriching her persona and strengthening her character, allowing her to prioritize societal connections over superficial relationships. Despite facing challenges, such as her daughter's rebellion, the heroine embraces these obstacles with acceptance and continues her quest for self-discovery. This journey illuminates the understanding that life is transient and that mental states are fleeting. She often finds solace in observing the trees outside her window, steady and nurturing, as she attempts to center her thoughts and regain stability amidst life's chaos. At times, the busyness of life disrupts her inner peace, and her energy wanes under life's myriad challenges. In those moments, even temporary escapes like alcohol fail to provide the relief she seeks, leading her back to introspection and nature's embrace. The refreshing breezes inspire her to sync her soul's rhythm with that of the natural world, urging her to delve deeper into her inner self.

The search for self is an intrinsic aspect of the human experience, representing the cyclical nature of existence. As the sun rises, winds blow, flowers bloom, and life flourishes in harmony with nature, humans stand out by possessing intellect yet often disrupt societal balance. Yet, this unquenchable drive for understanding one's existence amidst an incomprehensible vastness fosters a longing within the soul, driving the search for meaning. We welcome your thoughts on the presented novel.

Ragini Prasad,
Udaipur, Rajasthan
Email: sohmrag@gmail.com

1

On the uneven paths of the village, the herd of cows and buffaloes ambled homeward, each accompanied by their young calves. Two decades later, Amrita found herself returning to this familiar place, now with her two daughters at her side. Saanvi, the elder, was pursuing her studies in college, while the younger, Tanvi, had just completed her twelfth-grade examinations.

Seated atop the roof of her elder brother Mahindra's house, Amrita gazed out at the village that had changed so much yet felt unmistakably the same. A flood of childhood memories washed over her, vivid and unyielding. She recalled her father returning each evening with a bag brimming with fresh vegetables, only to sneak away to the nearby fields to visit Sakta, the local farmer, for a bottle of his homemade liquor. He would hold that bottle tightly, concealing it behind his back as if trying to shield it from prying eyes.

The giggles of Amrita and her siblings often filled the evening air, merging with the scent of kerosene lanterns as they poured over their chemistry and physics books. Each of them harboured dreams of becoming great scientists like Madame Curie or Einstein. Amrita, particularly captivated by a portrait of Madame Curie, used to ponder her fair complexion, whimsically dubbing her the "third stone." In village vernacular, a third stone was deemed useless, often dismissed even for practical tasks, like propping up a broken bullock cart. Yet Amrita held a soft spot for that third stone; in the rain, it would gleam and roll delight fully in the puddles. After each downpour, she and her friends would venture out in search of these smooth stones, eager to play the beloved “third stone game.”

As her thoughts drifted, Amrita’s attention fell upon a girl standing on a neighbouring rooftop, a girl who bore a striking resemblance to Urmila, her childhood friend, Urmila’s niece, perhaps? Her features mirrored those of Urmila: full lips, a small nose perched between petite eyes —but this girl’s teeth remained hidden, unlike Urmila’s.

“Urmila won’t be at school today,” announced Gunamala, hurrying off to class at the crack of dawn.

“What do you mean? There’s no way, Urmila who never misses a day, would take a holiday!” Amrita exclaimed, adjusting her book hat with both hands.

“She got married last night,” Gunamala replied, her laugh bubbling over. Her cheeks dimpled, and Amrita found the sound infectious.

“The baraat arrived from the nearby village and left at dawn.”

In a small village, Amrita was often the subject of whispers and judgments cast by her friends, who deemed her naïve and inexperienced when it came to the intricacies of marriage. They believed that the realm of bangles, bindis, anklets, lehengas, and odhanis was far too complex for her comprehension. Amrita belonged to a family that had migrated from a distant city, a place where she had only been taught the basics of reading and writing.

Her mother is educated," Urmila’s mother would remind her husband each year as another milestone of ignorance passed them by.

"If only my parents had given me an education, I could have been teaching in a school too," she would often lament to Amrita’s mother, whom she affectionately called Jiji.

"They never let me do a job," she would continue, her eyes reflecting the weight of her words. "They told me my duty was to care for the home and children. Here I’m a daughter of a Bohra family from UP, exiled to this barren village, where we have no sweet treats or fresh fruits to enjoy. I made this sacrifice for my children."

These words were familiar to Amrita, having often been shared by her Jiji, who was educated in a convent. Each evening, as Jiji sang “Om Jai Jagdish Hare” with her brothers and sisters, Amrita would ponder what God truly was.

She had always felt a strange sense of dislike toward the images of Lakshmi adorned with jewels in the glass paintings. The temple, filled with numerous deities, was Jiji's sanctuary; she had seen her conversing with those images, laughing in one moment and weeping the next.

She weeps perhaps because of the distance from everyone due to father's job," Amrita thought to herself as she noticed her Jiji's eyes glistening with tears. She recalled a letter that was to be sent to her uncle, slipped quietly into letter-box. After a recent argument with her father, her emotions boiled over, and she understood her silent need to express herself; she placed the note into the letter-box.

"I've severed ties with my brother too," Jiji remarked while serving food to her husband, "Whatever happens is what the God has planned."

"Patience is necessary. Boys and girls are getting educated now; we can't hold her back that way."

Amrita felt as if she could hardly breathe, pressed against the wall behind the door. The discussions clearly revolved around her elder sister, Badi Didi (Elder Sister), who hadn't visited in what felt like ages. Amrita missed her terribly; Badi Didi had once filled their home with laughter and stories before leaving for work and never returning. Whenever people in the village inquired about her absence, Jiji would merely fall silent.

Amba Uncle frequented Amrita's home,

sharing tales of the Ramayana, Gita, and Mahabharata. While smoking a mixture of lime and tobacco, he would chat for hours with Jiji, but Amrita often perceived an odd stillness in him when Jiji was around.

"Oh! Living here has turned me into a drinker," Jiji would sigh, "In this state, everyone is backward; life revolves around mere eating, drinking, and sleeping." Time and again, she would shield her husband, while Pandit Uncle sipped tea in silence, his small eyes narrowing even further after partaking of bhang.

The mere sight of Jiji's prasad would make his mouth water. Amrita couldn't help but smile; even now, the sweet scent of Atte Ka Halwa (Flour Pudding) would waft through her memories from time to time.

As friends moved away to their in-laws around the ages of twelve or thirteen, Amrita remained solitary in school. Her slender form felt far from the expectations of adulthood. In the evenings, as she lay on her bed in the courtyard, gazing up at the stars glittering in the night sky, she felt the stirrings of a different life—a world beyond the confines of marriage, deities, temples, and evening hymns. She found herself drawn to those who lived in the shadows, the dark-skinned workers who inhabited their homes, discarded leftovers as meals, donned ragged clothes, and wore smiles amidst their yellowed teeth. As she matured, the realities of bonded labour and the Mautana Dawari system began to unfurl before her, shrouded in layers of complexity that tugged at her youthful heart.

□

2

The world of college awaited Amrita in the bustling city—a land so far removed from her quiet village. Each morning, the sounds of her Babuji (father), battling a persistent cough mingled with the early whispers of the BBC tuning in to the day's news.

"Amrita, get up! The bus won't wait for you. I've made tea; drink it before you head out!"

At the sound of her mother's gentle yet urgent call, Amrita's drowsiness evaporated like morning mist. She would traverse the narrow village path, her heart set on the vibrant city beyond.

"Look at that girl; she comes all the way from the village to study!" The cyclists' comments floated in the air, their laughter a backdrop to Amrita's journey. Boys who had studied together in the same class for three to four years would share their experiences as if they had been on a mission to the moon—an impossible feat—rather than just completing their college studies.

In the tribal area where she lived,

challenges were many, but her father often reminded her, "Real strength is to rise above hardships." Those words, spoken by Babuji as he read the newspaper in the afternoon sun, illuminated Amrita's path, spurring her towards the light of possibility.

"Why do you go to college dressed like that?" her middle aunt chortled, pinching the end of her saree into her mouth, laughter bubbling forth like sparks igniting flames in Amrita's ears. She felt a deafening silence envelop her.

"Would you drink some tea, Auntie?" she asked, offering her aunt a cup, her heart pounding.

"Yes, dear," the aunt, taken aback, stifled her pride momentarily, accepting the offering as if it were a peace treaty.

"How many girls are in your class?" as Amrita's father approached, her aunt casually draped her saree over her head.

"I'm the only girl in my class," Amrita replied, pride and trepidation intertwining within her.

"Really! Alone among the boys?" her aunt's eyes glimmered with skepticism

"Yes, Aunt, there are ten or twelve boys."

"Just how old are you?" The inquiry pierced through the air as she took a sip of her tea, her gaze scrutinizing.

"Just about fourteen," Amrita said quietly, estimating her current age. She thought about the long two years she still had to wait before she'd be eligible to take her tenth-grade exams—not any earlier than that.

Aunt's eyes widened, momentarily reclining into worry as she said to Amrita's mother, "Take care of her; she's growing up!"

"She is but a girl focusing on her studies; we're not worried about her," her mother responded, wrapping the aunt in a warm embrace as she bid farewell. Yet, Amrita felt the sting of judgment for simply being a girl, a label that seemed to entrap her in shadows.

"Mummy, I have so many dreams to chase. Will you support me in pursuing my studies?" she implored, wrapping her arms around her mother, inhaling the faint scent of tobacco that both soothed and strengthened her resolve.

"Pass this class, and I'll stand by you, no matter where your education takes you next," her mother promised, her voice gentle yet unwavering. Amrita's heart soared with hope, as the thought of stepping onto a college campus, where she could belong and thrive, filled her with excitement and determination.

"You should aim to be like Indira Gandhi! She is the Prime Minister and has paved so many paths for women," her mother said, eliciting a hearty laugh from Babuji. Amrita joined in the laughter, her spirit soaring.

"Babuji, have you ever met Indira Gandhi?" she quizzed, startling him from his reading; while he'd encountered Nehruji, Indira remained a figure of distance.

"Why yes, she's my sister!" he declared playfully, placing the newspaper aside, and a lively discussion about the freedom struggle ensued—a tale that seemed infinite. Yet, Amrita felt the pangs of hunger, surrounded by her siblings, all eagerly awaiting the end of their parents' chat.

"I have to study tonight; I have an exam in the morning. Did you fix my bicycle's flat?" Mahindra asked his younger brother, as the household buzzed with thoughts of study and school.

"Everyone, wash your hands and come eat; food is ready!" their mother's voice rang out from the kitchen, drawing them all toward the warmth of home, where the enticing aroma of dal-bhaat lingered, promising comfort and nourishment for both body and soul.

□

1

Baba, the wise old grandfather, attended the wedding of his elder grandson, Mahindra. His heart swelled with joy at the sight of Amrita.

"Come along, my dear. There's a college not far from here where Neetu and Ranu study. You ride with them every day in a rickshaw!" Baba suggested, sensing a hint of discomfort in her demeanor.

Reluctantly, Amrita followed him to a grand old house with a long hallway and a Neem tree that proudly stood in the center of the courtyard. Though the rugged terrain of Chambal loomed nearby, the bustling city was alive with a cacophony of voices and palpable warmth. It was a place steeped in tradition: women veiled their faces while men donned towels draped over their shoulders. Many of the local men, after a long day at work, were often seen in their striped underwear, a casual nod to the heat.

As the rickshaw rattled along the streets, Amrita noticed that the girls around her kept their heads down, which puzzled her. Curiosity bubbled within her. Why did they bow their heads? Was it out of modesty or fear? Sometimes, she would sneak glances at the corners of the streets, wondering about the whispers she had heard about the notorious 'Bediyon Ka Mauhla' (The locality of Bedis' cast). What lay hidden in the shadows? She was determined to uncover the truth behind those secrets.

"Amu peeps a lot in the rickshaw!" Neetu remarked, sharing a chuckle with Badi Bua (Father's elder sister) who had taken care of Baba ever since becoming a widow shortly after her own marriage. Badi Bua always made sure to keep an eye on the old man, ensuring he ate well and remained happy.

"Be careful, Amu, don't go too far in your rickshaw escapades," Badi Bua warned, standing humbly with a glass of milk, recognizing Baba's tempestuous nature.

"In the morning, we'll take the bus instead," Neetu declared one evening as they prepared for bed, wrapping herself in a sheet.

"A closed-window bus will stop all the peeping eyes," Ranu chimed in, tucking herself in too. Amrita felt a wave of nausea at the mention of those prying eyes.

"Who are these people? What are they saying?" she drifted off to sleep, her mind swirling with questions. The next morning, the bus ride felt exhilarating, though the windows were tightly shut —a fortress against the outside world.

When a girl attempted to open one, the driver firmly reminded her, “The principal has forbidden it. You don’t want to attract attention here; we’re in a city shadowed by ravines, home to dacoits wielding guns,” a girl’s voice quipped from the back, sending shivers through the crowd.

The other girls fell silent, but Amrita felt a thrill of curiosity surge through her. What if she could meet one of those dacoits? Surely, they were mere humans with their own stories. She clutched her books close, staring into the void of her thoughts.

That fateful day, the college bus encountered trouble, leading Neetu to declare, “We’ll have to walk home.”

“You will be able to walk!" Ranu exclaimed, her little bright eyes shining with excitement.

“Has she returned from some foreign land? She'll walk all right! But that fair skin of hers will surely darken. Being too fair doesn’t mean anything if one lacks values,” Neetu quipped, a hint of teasing in her voice.

The remark stung, though Amrita wasn’t entirely sure why. Perhaps it was because of Umesh, the boy from the neighborhood who often cast sidelong glances at her while pretending to tend to his pigeons.

“Stay away from him, Amrita! He’s a pigeon fancier,” Anita warned her one day. “Just yesterday, I had to cycle to college. My brother sent me with Umesh, and that creep had the nerve to touch my hair while I sat awkwardly. It was infuriating!"

Amrita's heart raced. "What did he say?" she pressed, her intrigue piqued.

"He claimed that my brother didn't know any better; a young girl shouldn't be sent off with a young boy. Can you believe it?" There was anger in Anita's voice, a simmering disdain for Umesh's onslaught of entitlement.

Amrita absorbed this information, her feelings toward pigeons and their keeper shifting. As the girls continued their conversation, they crossed a rugged stretch of road, when suddenly; a heart-wrenching cry pierced the air.

"Perhaps someone is in danger!" Neetu gasped, fear in her voice.

"Maybe it's a girl trapped or sold into a life she can't escape," Ranu whispered, trembling.

"I have to see!" Amrita felt an unexpected rush of courage.

"No!" Neetu pulled her back urgently. "This is Bediyon Ka Mauhla. You might never return! What will we tell our families?"

Both sisters grasped Amrita's arms, hurriedly escorting her away from the cries that echoed in her heart. Against her will, she allowed herself to be led away, her gaze lingering on the homes hidden among the bushes, where lives were ensnared in a web of despair.

The cries faded, replaced by the soft rhythm

of anklets, setting a sorrowful melody against the tabla's beats. Tears streamed down Amrita's cheeks as she was dragged along, her heart heavy with the weight of another's plight.

Later that evening, secluded in her room, Amrita felt more alone than ever. Neetu came to her with a plate of warm rice and lentils.

"Eat something," she urged softly, feeding her despite the Amrita's earlier silence.

"I'll have a court marriage," Amrita declared, passion igniting her tone. "I'll refuse to conform to customs and dowries! I want something real!"

"Sleep now, you wild dreamer," Neetu replied with a smile, stepping out but leaving a part of her heart behind with her sister, both bound by unbreakable sisterly love and shared burdens.

The next year Amrita returned to her parents.

□

4

Beautiful fair Amrita had now completed her schooling. Amrita was very keen to study in college. Her parents also wanted that Amrita should study in college so that she could get married in a good family, but her elder brother Mahindra, did not want her to study in college at all.

"Colleges have opened; Amrita will now go to college to study." Babuji was talking to Mahindra while standing in the courtyard. Mahindra did not say anything but Amrita understood the lines drawn on his face. She was standing behind the door with her long black eyelashes lowered and was rubbing her dupatta (Long scarf).

"Babuji, the times are not good. What else should a girl know except basic reading or writing?" Mahindra said in a harsh tone.

Mahindra lived in the city for four years to pursue further studies, but he did not appear for the exams even for a single year. Every time he would come home before the exams making an excuse. Babuji would get very angry, but he would not go to appear in the examination. How many colleges had he changed in those four years? The same brother was stopping Amrita's studies today!

Mother was sitting on the ground muttering mantras while holding a rosary of beads. The sound of the mantra was very captivating. In the mantra, "Om Namah Shivaya" was echoing as 'Vaikhari - The Divine Voice' (A divine voice). Amrita's mind was slowly becoming calm. She stopped kneading her dupatta with both hands and went to her room and took out books from the cupboard and started flipping through them. She was a brilliant student in school. Her handwriting was like pearls. Once mother had told her that chanting mantras makes our life simple and honest. 'Vaikhari - The Divine Voice' takes our life to a different level, where life and the search for the life begin.

"But I'm unable to understand what you're saying." Amrita used to say while hugging her mother.

With a contemplative look in her eyes, Mother would shift her tone to one of gravity and say, "Every mother teaches her children the ways of the world, but only a rare few create a bond that bridges the spiritual and the earthly. Those children are indeed blessed, for they carry with them a connection gifted by their mothers."

Amrita would dash off to her bed, giggles on her lips, but the significance of her mother's words would wrap around her heart like a reassuring embrace, leaving a dazzling warmth in its path.

It was Amrita's third year in college. Brilliant Amrita was about to top the university, but she would often feel bored while studying, whenever she would see her classmate Amit in college. She would feel a tickling sensation as soon as she saw Amit. Her eyelids would become heavy and a river of hot blood would start flowing in both her ears. They would exchange smiles from a distance, but there was a pause after that. She also wanted Amit to talk to her, after all, how long would he keep making her blood boil by smiling from a distance.

Amit had also fallen in love with her beauty and was looking for a suitable opportunity to talk to her, but he was not getting the courage to talk to her. Perhaps due to the fear that she might reject him, he would feel happy just by seeing her from a distance. But one day he made up his mind that he would definitely talk to her.

That day, after getting free from class, Amrita came to the verandah and thought that let's go to the lawn because this entire period will be free and forty minutes will pass easily there.

“Amrita, would you join me for a cup of tea?" Amit inquired, stepping forward as soon as she took a step ahead, blocking her path with a warm smile.

Amrita was shocked by this unexpected question. For a few moments, she could not think what to answer. She did not expect that Amit would suddenly offer to have tea, but how could she say yes so immediately!

She said in a hurry, "I've some work with my friend, sorry!" saying this, she quickly went to the other side.

Amit was a little disappointed, but he thought that girls do not mingle so easily when they talk for the first time. He thought of trying again some other day.

It was two days later. Amrita was sitting in the library reading a book when Amit came and sat on the seat next to her.

"Hello!" Saying this, Amit extended his hand towards her.

Amrita smiled and extended her hand forward. After shaking hands, she again started pretending to be busy with the book.

Seeing her silent, Amit asked, “Will I have the privilege of having a cup of tea with you today?”

She also wanted to talk to him today, so she said with a light smile, “Okay!”

Both of them came to the college canteen and sat on the chairs placed next to the table near the window. While drinking tea, Amrita kept looking at Amit from time to time. Amit's personality had stolen her peace.

After that day, their meetings started increasing. Both of them would choose a secluded place in the college and share their romantic sweet nothings. Amrita started liking Amit's touch and Amit was on cloud nine after getting Amrita. That day, both of them were sitting together for a long time near the wall behind the college. Their conversation was not ending. She was lost in Amit's words.

After quite a while, with great difficulty she controlled herself and reached home, then she was terrified by her brother's roar.

"Where are you coming from so late?" Mahindra was saying while grinding his teeth. Her parents had also come to the courtyard. Amrita started crying while hugging her mother. Babuji went inside the house. Babuji was quietly listening to his son, but did not say anything. Babuji knew that his son did not like Amrita going to college. There must have been some reason.

"You stop going to college from tomorrow! It's over now," Mahindra was shouting. He went out in anger. Father sat quietly on a chair in the courtyard, exhausted. He had suddenly lost his mental peace.

The next day was somewhat calmer. Brother and father were very happy today. Mother was also making kachoris (A kind of salty fast food). Lots of fruits had also come home. Mother had applied mehendi on her feet today, and was also wearing a beautiful shiny saree. Her both hands were full of colourful bangles.

"Jiji, what festival is it today?" Amrita said

to her mother after seeing everything. Her college had been closed for a few days, but she had started going to college again, with strict instructions from Mahindra.

"Today is not a festival, silly girl; people are coming to see you!" Mother said laughingly but Amrita was shocked. She burst into tears. She should have asked her before doing all this!

"No Jiji, I don't want to get married!" Amrita burst out in anger. She started stamping her feet and crying.

"You don't want to, but we have to," Mother said while arranging a bouquet of flowers on the glass table.

Tears were flowing from Amrita's eyes. Today, mother was also treating her like a stranger! She started sobbing.

"Go and get ready, guests are coming to see you," Mother said while caressing her, and she went to her room making a face.

She was getting ready reluctantly. She was crying repeatedly, but there was no one to listen to her. After all, how can someone treat their daughter like a stranger like this? That too for a person whom she doesn't even know!

"Amrita, wear a Banarasi saree and put two bangles on your hand. Also wear a red bindi, guests are about to come," aunt said while looking at the clock on the wall. Mother quickly brought a red Banarasi saree and blouse for Amrita in her room.

“Take this and wear it, my Ammu, you’ll look like a princess!” said mother while giving her saree blouse and bangles.

Her eyes were vacantly fixed on her mother. With a smile, she left.

Amrita became more annoyed with her mother’s smile. How can Jiji smile like this when she is crying! Her mother had told her that they will come at six in the evening. It was only four o’clock. She was remembering Amit again and again. What will happen to him! He loves her more than his life. Due to fear of Mahindra, she had not even asked anyone about Amit.

Her restlessness was increasing due to the hustle and bustle of the house. She felt as if preparations were being made to kill her as a scapegoat!

Finally the moment came when the guests arrived. Mother sat on the floor and straightened the folds of Amrita's saree and said, "Fix your face a little; it looks as if you are going to do the duty of crying." Amrita went to the bathroom in anger. She had locked herself in the bathroom! Mother had coaxed her so much, and then she came out with great difficulty with her pale face.

"Jiji, you do puja-paath (religious rituals) and chant mantras every day, that’s why you got a good daughter like me who obeys everything you say," Amrita said, staring at the floor. Slim and fair Amrita was blooming in a Banarasi saree. She was looking even more beautiful wearing bangles, and the red bindi (forehead decorative dot) on her broad forehead had made her face more beautiful.

Mother just smiled looking at her, "Yes, only the lucky ones get daughters like you."

"Jiji, you say that mantra is vaikhari, and then what is vaikhari?" Amrita widened her kohl-lined eyes and spoke. Today Amrita's life energy was weakening; perhaps that's why questions were arising in her mind. When the mind is weak, it doubts a lot and something similar was happening with Amrita.

"Divine voice is what vaikhari signifies! Very good voice, that is. vaikhari is what happens when mantras pour out of our deepest selves and take the form of sounds. Mother said as she sat on the floor and smoothed Amrita's saree's folds.

Mother emerged from the room to greet the visitors as the doorbell rang. Amrita's heart pounded more rapidly. Her throat felt dry even after she poured the glass of water on the table and drank it all at once.

Amrita was sitting with that unidentified young man, their heads bent, face to face. They were not conversing. She sank into the sofa out of embarrassment. That young man wanted to say something, but when he saw Amrita's contempt for him, he remained mute. There was a large gap of silence between the two.

"How much have you studied so far?" the young man finally asked, breaking the silence.

She did not say anything.

"Son, have some sweets." Mother had brought a plate of sweets. Amrita felt relieved when her mother brought sweets. It felt as if a calamity had been averted! Her silence had told her mother everything. But, mother became restless. On one hand, there was the family tradition, and on the other hand, there was the educated daughter's own decision and future. The mother, who never stepped out of the house, had no choice in Amrita's favour, except to tolerate the conservative mentality of her husband and son. Now the same was going to happen to her daughter, killing her wish!

The guests had liked Amrita, but seeing Amrita's expressions, her own family members were worried.

□

5

The next morning, Amrita woke up and told her mother that she would go to college that day as her exams were approaching. Without caring about anyone's permission, she went to the college. She met Amit outside the library. He looked very tired.

"Why are you not coming to the college for so many days? Did your family make you quit your studies?" he came close and whispered in Amrita's ear.

She was crying bitterly.

"I understand everything. Let's sit and talk comfortably," saying this, they went to the library.

"What is your decision Amrita?" Amit's voice was very serious.

Amrita began sobbing as she declared, "I won't marry anyone but you. I only want to be yours." Her sobs filled Amit's heart too.

"Then it's okay. We both will get married, but make sure not to leave each other under any circumstances," Amit said, lifting her chin.

Amrita nodded in agreement with moist

eyes. She was seeing a firm determination in Amit's eyes.

As soon as the exams were over, Amrita told everyone about her decision to marry Amit. There was chaos in the house! Mahindra had broken many household items in anger. Father had become very weak and mother had become like a deaf and dumb person.

“Jiji, you’re the one who has spoiled her!" Mahindra lashed out at Mother, while Aunt arrived with her children."

"Yes Bhabhi, Babua (boy) is right. You should have taken good care of her. You’ve been too lenient with her. Now how will we face the society?" Aunty was wiping her tears with the pallu of her saree. Mother was sitting silently, her eyes fixed on the ground. Amrita had imprisoned herself in the room.

"Amrita won’t go out of the house now," Mahindra had gone out after making an open announcement. No one could do anything against his decision. Amrita did not say anything out of fear.

She thought about her decision many times, but every time, her heart would overpower her mind, and her mind would shut down. She started feeling as if this was destiny's wish. Finally, one day, she left the house secretly. Before leaving, she had left a letter saying that no one should try to find her. She was going to marry Amit, and she had made this decision after thinking it over and over again.

When the family came to know about this marriage, everyone sat down holding their heads. Mahindra showed his anger and said that he would teach them a lesson, and then mother warned him that if anything happened to Amrita and Amit, he would see her dead! Finally, everyone sat down quietly.

Breaking all the shackles of the world, both of them got married in court and came to the city.

After many days, Amrita's parents came to meet her, but they still had a slight resentment about the marriage. The mother's heart was filled with affection for her daughter, so even the father had to come along with her.

"Jiji, I've done nothing wrong. Times have changed now. Bhaiya (brother) will also get married if he gets some work."

"Ammu, how will he ever face society again? You should come home with us," her father said, his tone carrying a desperate plea.

"No, Babuji, I'm now Amit's wife and I cannot leave him. I reached this decision after careful consideration."

When Amrita announced her decision, Parents returned the next day. Time kept moving at its own pace. Slowly Amrita's family accepted Amit. Amit's family had only his mother while his father had passed away long ago.

At first, Amrita was thrilled to marry Amit,

but she gradually realized that a marriage without family approval could be more of a curse than a blessing. As she matured, this understanding became clearer. Neither the court marriage nor the inter-caste relationship provided her the peace she had expected. It was only after her marriage to Amit that she truly grasped how friendship and marital companionship could be worlds apart. Of course Amit was very good, but people are not able to digest a woman's own existence!

Gradually, her interest in politics started increasing. Amit had no likes or dislikes in this matter. He just wanted a settled household and she was a perfect fit for his household.

◇◇

"There is a great photo of bhabhi ji (Brother's wife) in today's newspaper," saying this, Raman took off his bag from his shoulder and placed it on the table. Amit had read the newspaper in the morning itself and the photo as well. He also knew about the meeting of the previous evening and the local news.

"Come in," Amit greeted Raman.

Amrita had also come out by then on hearing Raman's voice. She felt a different kind of tension on the face of Raman who was talking about Karl Marx. After greeting him, she sat down.

"What made you think of politics? Don't you know how those people are?" Amit was shocked by her bitter tone.

She was also surprised. She had not seen anything like this. Besides, she had just become a member in the party. She had been made the leader of the women's group only the day before. There was nothing there that would hurt her identity. She ran her hand over her neck, everything looked fine. The gold chain was in its place, the ear tops were in their place.

Everyone had tea together. While leaving, the newspaper photo was discussed again. She was laughing, but Amit's face had changed its colour.

After a long time, she and Amit had come to the park for a walk in the evening. A person coming from the front shook hands with Amit. Looking at Amrita, he said, "Ma'am, Namaste!"

She also replied to the greeting.

"Is she your wife?" he asked softly.

Amit started laughing.

"Yes, my legal wife too," Amit said laughing.

"Do you get time for politics and household affairs?" That person started looking at him with strange eyes.

"Yes, one has to make time. Life is not just about household affairs; there is life beyond this as well," while saying this, she started thinking that she sees the light of life only where hungry and thirsty people need two meals a day and children suffering from the heat need the shade of schools. Also, women need social security. Perhaps this is what she had come to this world to do. Unknowingly, she felt as if this was the purpose of her life.

He left after saying this but created a wall between her and Amit.

“Come, let's go and do some shopping from the shop in front,” she probed Amit's mind. She knew that his mood was spoiled, but she had asked him to test his mood.

“No, some other time.” Amit was not expressing his irritation even though he wanted to. Both of them returned home. As soon as he came, Amit started lighting a cigarette. Amrita was confused by the smell of cigarette.

"What is this? Why do you smoke so many cigarettes? Go outside and smoke," she said angrily, as both daughters walked in. Amit started watching TV without answering.

“Mummy was not at home even today,” Tanvi was crying in Amit's lap.

“When I came, the door was locked; even the aunty living nearby did not open their gate. Earlier she used to open it, but ever since she had a fight with Mummy, she doesn’t open it now.” The younger daughter's throat was choked with sobbing; that's why she hugged Amrita as soon as she came. But Amit...! There was tension and complaint on Amit's face. She quietly went to the kitchen. A lot was happening deep inside between her and Amit. The simple working Amit had understood her ambition. Her ambition was the light of her life. She was worried not for just one or two people but for many families. She wanted to absorb every pain but did not want to deviate from her purpose.

After she entered politics, there was a lot of discussion in this small town, but she was unaware of it and was busy with the cleanliness drive, the education drive, and running small industries for women in the slums around the city. Wherever she would go, there would be an exchange of greetings. Everyone in the party had become crazy seeing her dedication. The public was very happy. She would solve every problem of the city. She understood that the answer to a problem is often found within the problem itself and doesn't need to be sought elsewhere. Meanwhile, there was a buzz at the party regarding the MLA ticket.

"I've heard that your name is being sent for the MLA post." Kanak Mal, said while grinning.

"Why not? She's the most qualified woman in the eyes of the party president," Khurana Sahab teased, his voice coming from behind.

"You're still young; do whatever you want. After five years, no one will care about you in the party," Gupta Sahab said, twirling his moustache.

All the women around were smiling at each other. His words struck like burning embers, and her eyes were filled with tears.

"There will be a meeting tomorrow. You'll have to tell us what you have done for the people of the city in the last five years," the party president was explaining to her in very soft words.

"Yes," she could only say this much.

All the people around her were standing with bated breath and staring at her. Their eyes were tearing her body apart. She was becoming unconscious.

"Candidates for MLA ticket should come to the meeting hall tomorrow at five in the evening; the minister is coming from Delhi to decide the candidates," when the party president said this, everyone started looking at each other.

"Hey, where are you off to? Hold on, you're getting a ticket tomorrow, but today you have to treat us to sweets!" With that, everyone surrounded Amrita. A smile spread across her face.

That night the party president's phone kept ringing every now and then but she did not pick it up. She understood very well the meaning of the phone ringing late at night. She fell asleep holding Tanvi in her arms.

The entire hall was jam packed. She was stunned to see the unfamiliar faces of the candidates. Many were industrialists, many were big businessmen and many well-groomed women from big families were with their supporters. Amrita was alone watching the scene there, searching for the light of her life. Her supporters who were with her till yesterday became someone else's overnight. She had heard about a divorced queen, but had not seen her. She had heard that she had a lot of wealth. She had connections with big people. She had no qualms about drinking beer and alcohol. She used to visit Goa to spend her holidays. She used to go for shopping abroad. She was also coming there today for the ticket.

"The central minister is coming in a little while," the announcement was being made on the mike.

"Priyamvanda ji is also coming," the person sitting on the seat next to her was talking to someone on the phone.

"How many times have you visited Delhi?" the person asked suddenly, turning to her with a muttered tone as he hung up the call.

“No, never, I’ve only served here,” she said in a flat voice. He was staring at Amrita.

She was wearing the most beautiful and expensive saree she owned. She wore modest jewellery to the meeting today, but it didn't seem like her appearance, attitude, or level of service mattered in this situation. This was a show off event for wealth rather than a meeting to discover the true light of life's dreams. A twinge of disappointment shot through her. She didn't like that the person sitting next to her was staring at her.

The minister had arrived. All the sounds had stopped. As soon as he arrived, a fair-skinned, very beautiful woman came smiling from behind, wearing expensive clothes and diamond bangles, perhaps she had come with him. Amrita started remembering the hunger, naked bodies and dirty people of the slums. The woman who had snatched the wealth of the slums and had smeared it with makeup started to irritate her. Everybody was counting their own work. When Amrita was asked, she was not able to break her silence. She was feeling dejected. She did not know why the shining nose-ring in that lady's nose started getting stuck in her breath. Her breathing was becoming slow.

"This is Amrita ji, whose name we have unanimously given for the post of MLA candidate," the party president was saying.

The whole hall was echoing with the name "Amrita-Amrita". The minister himself was clapping. The lady sitting next to him was also slowly and delicately tapping the table, but the nose-ring in her nose was not shining as much now. Amrita looked around, the makeup of the women with lipstick on had faded and the faces of the famous people of the city had also become pale. Various kinds of sounds were coming. She was becoming empty.

□

6

Amit's excitement was palpable as he glanced at the door and saw Amrita walk in. His face broke into a wide grin. "Amrita, you have no idea, I've been waiting for you!" he said, his voice full of anticipation. "But before we talk, there's a group of journalists waiting for you in the drawing room," he pointed out, motioning toward the hallway.

Amit's face shone with an ethereal brilliance, reminiscent of a full moon illuminating the night sky. Yet, beneath the surface of that radiant smile, Amrita felt a storm of fear brewing within her. The journey of contesting elections was daunting—a formidable challenge, especially for a woman like her, who found herself an outsider in the male-dominated world of politics. With the weight of expectation pressing down on her, Amrita's head began to spin. The moment she entered the venue, a flurry of journalists converged around her, eager to capture her every word. Dazzling camera flashes erupted like fireworks, momentarily blinding her and thickening the air with tension. As she navigated through the barrage of questions, exhaustion washed over her, a relentless tide that seemed to pull her under.

"You're the first woman candidate of this constituency, what do you think about women?" a journalist was asking.

"I'll work for women in every field," she said very confidently.

"What will you say about these daily rape incidents?" another journalist asked and she got irritated.

"Women shouldn't be raped. The police will have to take action. I'll form a separate committee for these cases," she was saying in anger.

"But the conviction rate in rape cases is very low; most of the cases are settled. Is this right?" when a woman journalist asked, she started looking around.

"I'm tired, we'll talk tomorrow," saying this, she slipped away from there.

Her heart raced as she stared wide-eyed at the flood of questions surrounding her. "What on earth do these people want from me?" A wave of perspiration clung to her skin, each drop a testament to her mounting anxiety.

"It's not so easy for women to work, but still you'll do it," saying this, Amit embraced her and she snuggled up in his side. Her head cooled down completely. She felt relieved. She remained clinging to him like that for a few moments without saying anything, without listening to anything. Amit was also completely calm.

A long time was spent in the election campaign. Amrita's family members could not eat or stay together in the house. Funding for the election was a big problem for her. The people providing the funds also had reasonable and unreasonable demands. Some would shamelessly say it in front of her while others would do it indirectly. On the other hand, some people who were investing were loyal to the party and were providing the money without any conditions, but it would get over soon, so she had to ask them again and again. Amrita was facing a strange situation which was completely opposite to her nature.

On the other hand, the Election Commission was repeatedly reminding her of the limit of expenditure. She used to think many times that it would be so good if the elections were held with the amount fixed by the Election Commission. But the ground reality was exactly the opposite.

Fed up with the increasing pressure of the demand for funds, she thought of taking the money without worrying about right or wrong. Slowly she was opening up. First, she started meeting them over dinner with bottles of beer. After all, she had to win the election. It was necessary to fulfil the conditions of those who had promised funding before the elections. The story did not end here; girls had to be called from slums at night. Sometimes there was a demand for girls of thirteen-fourteen years of age. The light of her life was dying out. She was surrounded by shackles.

"A lot of dirty things are being said, you should leave this election," Amit tried to explain to her, but she was not going to listen to that inebriated voter. She was intoxicated with power along with the intoxication of the wine.

"You keep quiet!" she shouted, intoxicated. "The central minister is coming tomorrow; tomorrow we'll also have to send a girl from somewhere," she blabbered. While blabbering, she collapsed onto the sofa.

It was morning. When she opened her eyes, she was shocked. Amit had gone to another city with both the daughters. There was a message from him on her mobile – 'I am leaving the city with my daughters. I will not let your bad influence fall on my daughters under any circumstances. Do not try to meet me, I will send the recording of last night to the media.'

Her head was getting heavy. The veins on her head were taut. The maid was standing with a cup of tea. "Have some tea, Madam!" the maid said, turning her face away. Perhaps she had smelled the stench of alcohol.

"Go to the kitchen!" saying this she moved towards the bathroom, but Amit's message was creeping into her body.

"Oh no! What have I done? Why did I say that? I've lost sight of my roots! My mind is in disarray." She began to scream, clutching her head with both hands. She wasn't aware of when she collapsed in the bathroom, her cries echoing around her.

When she opened her eyes, she was in the hospital. Amit was standing near her bedside with both the daughters. Both the girls were looking at her, frightened.

"Mummy!" saying this, both of them started crying while clinging to her. Amit was still standing with his face turned away, he was very angry. She had done such a thing.

Shame, Shame! She hated herself. Due to the effect of the medicines, she slept again. By the evening, she had become normal. There was a slight injury on the head due to the fall.

"Sorry! I apologize; I wasn't able to concentrate in intoxication," she was apologizing to Amit, but he was not normal. After all, no father can become normal after such a cheap thing, never. She understood. She had made a big mistake. She was scared of the daily fair and unfair demands of the leaders who came from outside to support her.

At last, she said to the president, her voice breaking, "I won't contest this election."

"I've staked everything on you, leaving no room for anything else. Millions of rupees have been bet on you. We can't back out now under any circumstances, understand! If you won't listen to the minister, then don't even talk about contesting the election. All the people in the party have manipulated for you," saying this, the party president pushed her hard. She hit the wall and regained her balance with great difficulty.

"Should I commit suicide?" she was thinking while sitting in her room at home. She was very depressed and looking for sleeping pills when the phone rang. She saw that it was a call from the minister.

"What are your plans for tomorrow night?" he asked, slurring his words from the effects of alcohol.

She started trembling after saying, "Sir... sir..."

"Cat got your tongue? Why aren't you saying anything?" the minister kept asking.

"Sir... Sir..." In a panic, the phone slipped from her hand. She burst into tears. She was crying loudly, trapped in the shackles. There was a crowd of people outside her house, but nobody could hear her voice amid the election slogans. Suddenly Pushpa Bai came and snatched the tablets from her hand. Amrita was crying in her lap.

"Be patient, everything will be fine. You have to win the election and come home, you have to defeat the men; then see, and everything is justified in the government. These men also do all this. How many times did the party president go to Delhi with his wife? Stop focusing on these unnecessary things and move ahead. Yesterday a thirteen year old girl gave birth to a son in the hospital; it's the handiwork of someone in the family, terrible Kaliyug!" Pushpa said this while holding both her ears with both hands. Hearing this, Amrita started crying again like an innocent child.

◇◇

The atmosphere in her home was thick with tension, as a multitude of doctors filled every corner. Yet, in this moment, Amit and their two daughters were noticeably absent. The familiar faces from the gathering lingered, their conversations hushed and serious. Outside, the world was gearing up for the elections just two days away, while within these walls, she was battling an unexpected illness that had cast a shadow over the impending excitement. The code of conduct had been imposed. But many wrongdoings were bound to happen in her presence. The minister Sahab was also roaming around her drawing room restlessly.

The doctor looked up after checking her pulse, concern etched on his face. "She's exhausted and battling depression," he remarked, his voice steady. "But apart from that, everything appears to be normal.

Everyone breathed a sigh of relief. She was lying on the bed and staring at the pictures of her daughters and husband hanging on the wall.

◇◇

The election results were to be announced today. There was a bustle in the election office since morning. Everyone's eyes were on the election results. She was also forgetting her sorrow in the announcement of the election results, but the faces of both the daughters were flashing before her eyes. Her eyes were filled with tears. She was tired of sitting on the sofa in front of the TV in the office.

She was physically in the office, but she was dying of guilt. Some evil people have left no stone unturned in bringing politics to its lowest ebb. How many compromises must women have to make in this service sector? Can people with bad attitude be expected to serve the public! Her heart was very sad. Victory or defeat had no meaning for her.

“Congratulations Amrita! You are moving ahead of everyone every moment,” saying this Usha held her hand, who had supported Amrita a lot all the time.

She was not moving ahead, she was going backwards in the past. When the mind goes back it remembers only bitterness, this is what is said about the mind. But, her mind was going towards her happy family again and again.

Today she was missing her mother a lot. “You’re lucky. You have two daughters each. Make both of them such that they do something for the society, for women and for the country. Everyone does marriages, eating, drinking, travelling and fulfilling worldly affairs, but being useful to others is the success of life," mother with a lot of vermilion in her white hair had said once.

"Indeed, indeed. You spend your days lecturing young girls, but tell me, what have you truly done for women?" Father's words dripped with sarcasm as he teased Mother.

"Pandit ji! I've sacrificed my life for you and your home. You never gave me a chance to go out of the house." Mother was fuming. Her face had become more vermilion than the sindoor (vermilion) in her white hair, like the full moon. The moon shines with borrowed light; a wife also shines under the protection of her husband.

Amrita smiled. The muscles of her face expanded as she smiled. Her tension was reducing. It is said that a child smiles four hundred times a day, fifty times when he grows up, and hardly anyone smiles when he becomes an adult. Her smile was increasing as she thought. As we grow up, our ego increases, we forget to smile. Even in such tension, the smile gave her relief.

◇◇

"Amrita Zindabad! (Long live Amrita!) Amrita Zindabad! Our leader Amrita Zindabad!" A wave of happiness over her winning the election had spread everywhere. Her trance had broken. She was laden with flowers and was being covered in bouquets, but the wave of victory was still on. Looking at the faces of many people, she felt that they were happy not with her victory but with the victory of the party. Even the unhappy faces were wearing a cloak of fake happiness, but she was happy and had forgotten everything; she could only remember her mother's face. Tears of happiness welled up in her eyes.

She was alone even in the crowd. There was a flood of new challenges in front of her and there was also the voice of opposition, but she was confident. This victory was a gift for her, which refreshed her life and gave her an identity in the society. She bowed down before everyone, but there was something inside that was yearning to come to the top. She had recognized it, it was her ego!

She was looking into the distant future with both her daughters. How can he keep her away from her daughters? He is not that innocent? He too had acquired the mines in some illegal way. This normal man did not become such a big businessman of the city in such a hurry. It was his downfall when he left her with the minister at the circuit house late that night. She kept calling him, but he did not stop. Finally, she returned home in the darkness of the morning.

She was walking with the crowd. She crushed the bunch of flowers lying on the way with her right foot. The men and women walking on her left and right were looking at her in surprise.

Someone shouted, “Amrita Zindabad!”

Everyone started shouting together again. Usha put her hand on Amrita’s shoulder. Both her shoulders and neck were erect. She was moving forward with straight steps. She was moving forward, breaking every obstacle that was in her way. Her gaze was steady, staring at the other side of the meeting hall where her aspirations were restless, to expand the limited sky. The sky of her aspirations had shrunk within her own limits.

◇◇

"You should have your meals on time," Usha was explaining to her. Her meal timings often fluctuated. Sometimes she would miss breakfast, sometimes lunch and sometimes dinner would be at 2 in the night. The same thing happened that day too. She was having lunch at 4 in the evening when Usha came. She quickly finished her meal and came back, but Usha had to wait for some time in the office.

Usha had life experience; she had been in politics for years. From the land mafia to small grocery shopkeepers, everyone saluted her. Many times she got tents of vegetable vendors installed on the empty spaces on the road, although she kept filling pages in the newspapers against encroachment, but her credibility in the party kept increasing. Wearing sunglasses, she used to take women from slums to big houses behind her flag.

Sometimes the sunglasses looked absurd on her dark complexion, but she considered herself very modern by wearing sunglasses. Wearing black complexion, sunglasses on top of it, a necklace of thick red pearls around her neck and a dark coloured saree, she looked different from everyone else. She used to work for women, but she did not do anything special for them, but yes, she used to get the photos of women printed in the newspapers by standing every big leader in the middle.

Usha's role was considered important in getting the land of journalist colony from the government. It was heard that the news about the clean image of the party among the public was published under her guidance, although her image among the public was not clean. Privatizing the media was her success and she was successful too. She used to sit in the front row in the events organized by religious gurus. She was a strong supporter of single women power and many organizations were also running in this direction under her supervision.

"Yes, I don't feel hungry, and then I don't get free from work. We've to bear the brunt of the mistakes of the previous government. There is so much mess in ration distribution. Roads were not built in the villages whereas the maps were passed and the contractors were also paid! How do I correct all this?" Amrita's disappointment increased while saying this.

Her challenges had become problems. The problems those were bigger than her existence. Her existence seemed dwarfed to her. She was falling apart. Everyone wanted to get their files done first. Everyone was in a hurry to get their work done and she did not have a magic wand. Twenty-four hours a day were not enough to do any work, and the body would also get tired and exhausted. Wandering around in the villages would make the feet stick to the mud, but no work could be done.

Usha kept staring at her! Usha herself wanted to get land allotted for her NGO, right in the middle of the city.

"Where are Amit and your daughters? Is there something wrong? They haven't been seen these days. I was thinking of asking them for many days!" Usha had sharpened her gaze towards him.

"Yes...they're just angry. I don't understand." She opened the files and started looking at them.

"Your family should take advantage of your status. You'll see that in a few days, relatives will come to you, the angry ones as well as the distant ones, the fake ones as well as the real ones!" She got up from her chair laughing.

"I'm leaving; I've to go to a meeting now. And yes, don't you get along with your MP?" Usha asked while getting up.

After becoming an MLA, she had acquired the art of tolerating the accusations that were made on her daily. Now she did not get upset over every small thing. She used to ignore the person in front of her, but she did not show it.

Usha had got up; Amrita started reading

the file with her head down. She paused for a few moments and then slowly left. She was watching her from behind.

“Hello!” when the phone rang, she said in a tired voice.

“Have the bills for the construction of the girls’ school building not been passed yet?” Khanna Sahab was saying.

“Yes, I’m getting that checked. The contractor has used very poor quality construction material. I’m getting it checked; I have a meeting with the collector today,” saying this, she switched off the phone.

◇◇

The police officers had stopped her car outside the collectorate. She was taken aback. It was important to meet the collector today.

"Madam, all the civil work contractors of the city are coming with a procession, you’ll have to wait," as soon as the police officer said this, she became suspicious. Mr. Khanna's call had come just a while ago. She had a file of construction material in her hand.

"I’ll go inside," she said and rolled down the windows of the car. Policemen surrounded her car from all sides. Slowly her car was moving towards the collectorate gate. She saw Mr. Khanna talking loudly to other contractors. She knew that the MP's sycophant did a lot of work for him, but she was not going to come under pressure, her confidence had increased a lot by staying with the public. She believed that women and their work do not get recognition at all. Not just women, no one does, but when we walk on the right path, people join us.

"The world is running because of good people, there are very few bad people. Some people can be bad, but not all," Babuji used to say. These days she was remembering every single word of her parents. She had become very lonely. It seemed that the whole world was filled with thorny bushes. Her feet were getting bruised and bleeding, but she had to walk, very far; where she could do something for the people. Every girl going to school was her inspiration and every woman was a source of energy for her. Keeping aside all the troubles, pain and obstacles in life, when women laugh, dance to the beats of dholak, (drum) it seems that these women have gathered the liveliness of the whole world in their lap.

She asked the collector to set up an inquiry committee.

"Ma'am, we've to make the payment," the collector said, peeking through his glasses. "We've got the work done, and then these people can go to court," the collector was trying to explain to her.

For the past several months, she had received several complaints of bribery by this officer. Rasik Lal had told her that the current collector Sahab was not honest. He hid big scams and blew small things out of proportion. Last month, the case of bribery in ration was completely suppressed, while hundreds of trucks were passing through the government warehouse in the dark of the night. Rasik Lal was a thin man. He would always come to Amrita with a piece of paan (betel) in his mouth. If the doorman or the PA stopped him, he would just say, "I've very important work with madam, I've to meet her right now, if I don't meet her, it will be a disaster."

He used to sit in the hall for hours, Amrita was told about his arrival after a long time. Everyone could tell from Rasik Lal whose news he had brought. Rasik Lal kept track of all the officers because he was in touch with them. Amrita knew that his information was accurate. Apart from Rasik Lal, Lal Mohammad had also said the same thing that day when she was coming out of the meeting at the collectorate.

"Ma'am, get him removed. He is useless, he doesn't do any work; he is just busy filling the coffers." Lal Mohammad had many other complaints about him. Lal Mohammad was very firm on his principles. He was honest and also committed to the party. He kept a watch in every way as to how and where the image of the party was being tarnished. He knew that in politics, the voter is the most important, and this is the basic principle of our constitution. Although Lal Mohammad was a small leader, he knew that democracy would be strengthened by giving importance to the individual.

"Madam ji, I believe that our society should

rise above the confines of caste and religion. When caste is misused, it can profoundly undermine the very foundation of our democracy." He had expressed this sentiment with care on several occasions, each time emphasizing the importance of unity and understanding.

Deep in her heart, she held an unwavering belief in his vision. Her eyes were set on the voters —the very lifeblood of politics. These were the voters she sought: those who revered the act of voting as their sole creed, determined to see their chosen candidate triumph. Her aspirations were simple yet profound; she yearned to be a steadfast ally to the voters, a guardian of their hopes and dreams.

□

7

That day, on her younger daughter's birthday, Amrita had gone to Amit's house. She had her whole group of musclemen with her. The Superintendent of Police had also come with his car. Now she had acquired many skills of life to get her point across without creating a ruckus.

"I can't imagine my life without children; they're all I really want," she had told Akash.

Akash was the biggest hotelier of the city. He had many hotels in the city and out of the city too. He was the epitome of wealth and success in the town. He owned a chain of luxury hotels, each more luxurious than the last. He wore designer clothes and sported a Rolex watch, a thick gold chain and several diamond rings. He owned several expensive cars, including a Rolls-Royce Phantom and a Ferrari. His lifestyle was a testament to his wealth and success, and he was known throughout the town for his extravagant taste. He had a charming and jovial personality. Once he organized a party for Amrita and after that they started meeting each other. He loved to live lavishly and so did Amrita. His wife lived in

America with their two daughters for studies.

"Amrita, is it alright if I call you Amrita?" Akash asked, gazing deeply into her eyes.

She liked the shining black mole under the gold chain around his neck. In hotels, under the glittering chandeliers at night, they would often come very close to each other and talk about the light of life. The love of a person of forty-five years is very mature.

Whenever she felt a flicker of doubt in their relationship, Akash would gently remind her, 'We're both here to help each other grow.' His words were a comforting assurance, a promise that together they could navigate any storm.

"You should leave all these things, just focus on your work." The light of the lamp coming from the thicket of trees was spreading on Akash's face. There was a lot of depth in his big black eyes. His eyelids moving up and down were the pause of an era for Amrita. Her era would stop and she would get lost in his company. She had a strange attachment with a stranger with whom she had no relation, but her heart was getting happy in every moment of his company.

"You want both the daughters, why didn't you tell me till now?" Akash said in a serious voice.

"Yes, I can no longer imagine life without my daughters. My breath falters, my soul aches when they're gone," her voice quivered, and she could hear the soft, pained sound of her own breaths.

Expensive sarees, expensive branded jewellery had no meaning for her now. They didn't have any meaning earlier either, but earlier the burden of comparison was on her mind; now she had come very far away from comparative observation in her personal life. Life passes just like that in comparing with each other and we get tied in each other's personality, get entangled in each other's flaws and goodness.

"I call SP Sahab right now; go tomorrow to get the children," Akash said, taking his phone out of his pocket.

"Hello, SP Sahab! You tell the Clock-Tower SHO to talk to me."

"Yes, I'll tell you right now." She could hear SP Sahab's voice sitting close to Akash.

◇◇

Throughout the night, she remained restless, turning in her bed. The prospect of seeing her daughters the following day, after so long time of separation, filled her with anxiety. She wondered what Amit had instilled in their minds.

"I never thought my life would become so unbalanced," she told Akash during a late-night phone call.

"You go to sleep Amrita, everything will be fine. We cannot say what will happen in life. We have to overcome the events." Akash was yawning while talking. Amrita looked at the ticking clock on the wall, it was 1 am.

After whispering 'I'm sorry,' she ended the call, yet the turmoil within her mind persisted. Her mind was entangled between right and wrong, but her ambition was becoming more and more unsatisfied. She did not know what else she wanted; she was not able to understand. She was getting away from the light lying in the dark pit. Print media, TV, meetings with big people were happening daily. Political turmoil had shaken her existence, but the pit of darkness was getting deeper and she was ready to jump into it. She had to save her political existence at any cost, but it seemed that its cost was increasing and her existence was getting smaller, even after sacrificing everything.

Today she experienced that the ticking off the clock in the dark night is very scary. The air conditioner, running at full power, was emitting a rather eerie noise. She felt that someone was near her. She got up from the bed suddenly. Her throat was getting dry, she had switched on the bulb, but no one was near. She was scared but could not figure out the reason for her fear. She sat for a long time with a glass of water in her hand, then gulped down the whole glass in one go. Now she felt a little relieved.

"How will I face my children and husband? I'm falling into the abyss day by day," she murmured to herself. The clock struck 3:30 AM. A wave of exhaustion enveloped her; her eyelids felt leaden, a tingling sensation flickered in her mind, and sleep appeared to be just out of reach.

She opened the window and started looking outside. The city traffic was moving slowly, but by the time the day broke, the traffic would increase - emitting smoke and carrying its blackness. “I had also moved at a slow pace in politics, but now my pace has also increased with my darkness, where I have ruined relationships and torn apart marital life,” she was mumbling. Everything is justified in political life, she had heard this many times in the meetings of political parties. In politics, everyone prepares himself to suppress the voice of his conscience. No one can escape from there, perhaps not even Amrita.

“But what have I done!” she muttered. She shook her head and started getting ready to go to her daughters.

◇◇

She reached Ram Nagar at eight o'clock in the morning. There were two police vehicles in front of her car; one vehicle was behind her car and two vehicles were behind it. As soon as the vehicles stopped, Amit came out trembling.

"Madam is here to take both daughters!" the driver said, leaning slightly out of the car window.

Amit's face went pale upon hearing this as he looked at the line of cars. He hurried inside and came back with both of his daughters. When both the daughters came to Amrita hesitantly, she opened the car door and spread her arms towards them. Both of them curled up in her arms like ducks.

"Let's go home, my dear," saying this, she took Tanvi in her lap. Both of them sat in her car in a state of fear, perhaps Amit had explained it to them. Both the daughters sat in the car like prisoners. A strange confusion had surrounded her. She couldn't meet the gaze of her elder daughter Saanvi, who was gazing out the car window. The three of them were feeling very distant even though they were together. Their suffocation had spread throughout the car. All three were lost in their own thoughts, connected to each other; but also isolated from each other.

◇◇

The morning dawn was hazy. The clouds were scattered and there was humidity too. The grey clouds were piercing again and again, covering the sky. The clouds were slightly black in some places and slightly white in others. She was getting confused. Neither the whiteness was pleasing to her, nor was the blackness pleasing to her mind. She was not able to understand anything. When she thought of a snake as a rope, it was actually a snake and when she picked up a rope thinking it to be a rope, it was actually a snake.

Thinking, she started panting. Dark

shadows were hovering around her. Relatives had come very close, but she was going that much farther. Everyone had their own calculations, their own standards and she was giving a trial by fire every moment. It was a trial by fire, yet she felt no heat beneath her feet; instead, her joyful emotions resided there. She watched as those feelings seemed to burn away beneath her, turning her very existence into a daunting challenge.

"Who am I? But really, who am I?" she asked herself, lost in thought. Saanvi's arrival brought an abrupt silence.

"Mummy, Papa called today," Saanvi said, holding her gaze.

It had been two days since Saanvi had come to her; today Amrita was overjoyed to see a smile on her face for the first time. Tanvi was becoming normal, but ever since Saanvi came, she could only see a series of questions in her eyes. How could she answer her unanswered questions, but today Amrita's mood improved due to Amit's phone call.

"Yes, what did Papa say?" Amrita asked, personally handing Saanvi a glass of milk. There were many kinds of cut and ripe fruits on the dining table. Seeing the table decorated with various kinds of fruit juices, Saanvi became happy and her cheerfulness brought excitement to Amrita's dejected mind.

“Papa is on his way to see you.” The moment Saanvi spoke those words; her ears began to feel warm. A blush, like a whispered secret, painted her cheeks. Inside, her heart performed a frantic drum solo, a staccato beat against the silence of her thoughts.

"So, he's coming now? Call him quickly, I have to leave again," she said while controlling herself. She did not want any nagging or bondage now.

When Saanvi mentioned, 'Papa said you're going to become a minister,' Tanvi began to applaud enthusiastically.

"My mother will become a minister!" And, she stood up while having breakfast and started dancing. Amrita was also laughing. All three of them were laughing. Pushpanjali was also laughing while giving Amrita a glass of milk.

"Ma'am, as soon as you become a minister, please get me a housing board home. I am tired of paying house rent, please do me this favour." She was standing in front of Amrita with folded hands. Seeing the line of sindoor in her black and white hair, she remembered the sindoor in her mother's completely white hair. The corners of her eyes became wet.

"Saanvi, if your grandmother were here today, she would have been so happy!" Amrita went forward and hugged Saanvi. She felt very relaxed by Saanvi's touch. There is a relationship between mother and child not only of blood, but also of soul. A soul has to unite two souls to come to earth. Children decide their parents in this world.

She started caressing her hair with her fingers. Her mother often used to say that when she was sad, she used to read Ramayana and Geeta; perhaps this is what was written in the scriptures.

She held Saanvi tightly in her arms. The daughter's gentle breathing brought a rhythm to her restless thoughts.

She kissed Saanvi's forehead, feeling a rare stillness within.

Maybe, like her mother, she too would find peace in quiet faith.

□

8

The morning breeze was blowing gently. Amrita was sitting in the lawn sipping tea while everyone else was still asleep.

Just then she got a call from her elder brother Mahindra on her mobile.

"Hello, Bhaiya," she chirped brightly.

“Come home once, you haven’t come for a long time. It’s been a long time since I met Saanvi and Tanvi, everyone misses you. Mahadev temple has also been built.” Mahindra laughed while saying this.

Amrita remembered that Mahadev temple was everyone’s favourite place in the village. At that place, all the brothers and sisters used to play, roam around and sit on the roof of the temple and dream about the coming tomorrow.

"Bhaiya, we've been looking forward to visiting the village for so long, and I'm thrilled you've finally confirmed it!"

“Okay, so when are you all coming?”

“Today itself, we’ll leave in a little while.”

Mahindra was happy. She woke everyone up and asked them to prepare for going to the village. In a short while, everyone was ready.

◇◇

Amrita had come to her village with her two daughters, carrying these memories, but now there was no charm in the relationships, the relationships had become flat like the bonsai trees planted in the small balconies of big buildings, which gave the message of their presence, but did not give fruits and fragrance. She took a deep breath.

"You are not well, Amu!" Mahindra looked worried.

"No Bhaiya, I'm fine. I'm a little tired," Amrita said yawning.

"You all get some rest; I'll return shortly, and we can chat," Mahindra said, heading out, presumably to meet his friends.

Mahindra wanted Amrita to meet all of his friends. All of Mahindra's village friends wanted to meet Amrita; after all she was the pride of the village. Mahindra, his friends and everyone in the village used to say the same thing. Earlier she used to be happy with such things, but now these praises were becoming a burden for her. She wanted rest, where she could pause for a few moments. Stop with the journey of oneness in her breath. Towards her existence which asked her

"Who am I?"

She yearned for a morning that was radiant yet soft on her eyes. She inhaled the crisp morning air, the moonlit chill lingering in her eyes as daylight broke. With each breath, she felt a sense of lightness, a chance to momentarily escape her daily grind. In that pause, her thoughts fell quiet—no one intruded, no one departed. She simply attuned herself to the soothing rhythm of her breath, embracing the stillness, free from longing and the cravings of her mind, immersed in that solitary search for peace.

For breakfast, Mahindra had ordered jalebi and kachoris from Lala Halwai. Often her tongue used to bite while eating kachoris with tamarind chutney made by Bhabhi (Brother's wife). She used to lose patience to eat kachoris because of the taste, but today nothing like that happened. Her mind was filled with carelessness. In carelessness, the mind gets filled along with the body; a strange heaviness comes in life.

"Eat kachori, Amu." Bhabhi had said so and Amrita's eyes fell on her face. Bhabhi's long pointed nose was no longer as long as before, it had become thicker from the front. Her eyes were also not as intoxicating as they used to be at the time of marriage.

"Yes Bhabhi, but I don't feel like eating kachori," she started crying while saying this. Mahindra slowly got up from his chair and started caressing her head. Bhabhi also came and stood near her.

“We also miss Jiji and Bauji a lot. If they both were here today, they would have been so happy to see you. They were so proud of their promising daughter,” Mahindra said in a tearful voice.

On hearing all this, she started sobbing, hugged her brother; she felt as if she had hugged her father. She could smell Bauji in brother's sweat. The crying had stopped, leaving only the small, rhythmic hiccups, and in that suspended moment, time seemed to hold its breath with her. Her unspoken sorrow had brought her very close to her soul and in sorrow she had come close to herself.

She slept deeply at night. Amrita was resting in the lap of sleep after a very long time; she slept very deeply without a drink. She did not remember a single dream of the whole night, otherwise every morning as soon as she woke up, she used to think about the dreams she had at night.

'Karaagre vaste Lakshmi, kar madhye cha Saraswati, kar moole tu govidam.' She could understand it’s real meaning well as : ‘At the tip of the hands resides Goddess Lakshmi, in the middle of the hands resides Goddess Saraswati, and at the base of the hands resides Lord Govinda’.

Her mind was very empty while reciting the mantra.

"For spiritual energy, it is also important for the mind to be empty, only then nature will enter someone. Milk can be taken only in an empty vessel; it cannot be taken in a filled vessel," Bauji used to say often.

"Don't think everything in your mind for the person in front of you," Bauji used to say this to Jiji during the banter between Jiji and Bauji.

"As is the vision, so is the creation!" Jiji also used to reply to Bauji with alacrity. Bauji would pick up the corner of his white dhoti, put it on his shoulder and go out to the veranda outside the house. He would sit quietly for hours with his chin in his hand, but jiji would get busy with her household chores after saying this.

'This is the sole distinction between a man and a woman. A woman is often seen as delicate, yet the more sensitive she is, the stronger she becomes! Conversely, while a man may be sensitive, he tends to be weak at heart.' Akash had remarked this after she had left him sleeping and returned from the Circuit House.

Akash had cried putting his head in her lap that day at Amrita's house. She had understood Akash's love and her loneliness for the first time, but she did not want to be bound. Her feelings were vanishing day by day. She aimed to stay involved in all city projects to ensure her influence endured and her position remained secure. She was becoming very ambitious. Only her wings were strong and powerful around her. She would pluck the weak wings with her own hands. There was no dearth of wings around her, she just had to choose the strong ones for her to fly in the dwarf sky of politics and fulfil her ambitions.

She had to go back today; it had been three days here.

"Come, let's all go to Mahadev temple, let's all seek blessings for you together." Mahindra was standing with a coconut with husks in his hand. Bhabhi was standing with a puja (worship) plate in her hand.

They all had come to the temple to have darshan.

"Didi ji, Namaste."

“As soon as you become a minister, come here first.”

All the people coming and going were greeting her with such voices, with their own advices. She was very happy. A kind of energy was flowing in her. The freshness of childhood memories was making her life flow towards her goal. She had also overcome her guilt by staying with Saanvi; perhaps she had forgiven Amrita.

Mahindra broke down in tears as she sat in the backseat of the car on the way back to her destination.

“You are Durga, you are Saraswati! This is my only blessing!” Mahindra burst into tears while saying this. Bhabhi's eyes were also filled with tears. Amrita’s eyelids also became moist.

□

9

Amrita returned to her city with a heavy heart along with her daughters. As soon as she reached the city, she got busy in her daily chores.

She now started meeting everyone and started sending birthday wishes to everyone. She had hired a person for this purpose only to contact the city's prominent citizens and all such persons who could garner as many votes as possible. She had to prepare a vote bank! She wanted to have such a deep relationship with the voters that every voter would be able to recognize her when the elections came. She wanted to build a personal relationship with every voter. As a mother, as a sister; she wanted a familial relationship. She also felt very lonely even though she lived with her full family. Many times she used to wonder how people spend their lives alone. Loneliness must be tormenting them. She had become used to the crowd of people around her who would always agree with her and also keep praising her. She wanted to expose herself too much in the society, to create a good image of herself. She really loved herself a lot, perhaps this was her nature too.

'Why do you need to run around so much? You have everything. Let's go to Goa and stay there for a week. The travel agency will make all the arrangements, even the night shift.' Kavita had said this many times with a meaningful smile. Despite having short bob-cut hair and two marriages, Kavita preferred to be called Miss. Even after two marriages, she did not have children who would get stuck somewhere in life; she would always keep wandering in search of happiness. At the age of sixty-two, she was always enthusiastic about maintaining her figure in the gym. Otherwise, she was into sports since childhood and her body-build was also good.

“No, I have to prepare for my election now. Anyway, I don't like to go like this. You’re my childhood friend, it doesn't mean that you say anything nonsense in front of me,” she said with a little anger and Kavita started looking at the fan.

"Yes, you go out roaming with Akash; who will take this old woman? I make my own arrangements. I’m very self-respectful in this matter,” she was saying this while running her fingers through her dyed hair and biting her teeth. She had shot a direct arrow at Amrita, but she remained silent, she did not want to make a big deal out of it.

Kavita had gone, but she had challenged her feelings and existence. Stretching her legs on the sofa, she was staring at the ceiling and listening to the sound of the fan. Even the sound of the fan was tiring her. She sat up and switched off the fan. As soon as the fan was switched off, she felt relieved and she closed her eyes and sat quietly. As soon as she closed her eyes, her mind was filled with many thoughts, but she remained sitting quietly. She had started understanding now that the thoughts coming to her mind do not exist.

◇◇

Every street corner of this city was known to her. The end of every street was a step for her rising step in politics. The courtyard of every house had blessed her, that's why she was able to win the election. Every community, every caste and every section of the society had faith in her and she was also connected to everyone with all her heart. There was great commotion when she visited the colony behind the Mazaar for her election campaign. Her party people had stopped her from going there, only because she could not meet her voters, while every vote was precious for her. In the last election, the big leader of the party had lost by just one vote. The case has been going on in the court for the last six years, now what is the use of winning! The second election had come. She wanted to collect every single vote for herself in the ballot box. She could only see the voters; everyone else was meaningless except the voters.

"The root of democracy is the voter; do not divide the voters on the basis of religion and caste. Remember we are the citizens of a democratic country, we have to save the democratic values," when Amrita addressed the crowd of thousands with a pallu on her head, the marquee resounded with thunderous applause. This was all she wanted. The thunderous applause satisfied her existence. She felt refreshed seeing the smiling faces of the people clapping. She knew that only a happy person can clap. Her people were happy with her, it meant everything was fine.

An angry person can never clap and even if he does, darkness is visible on his face. While clapping, we are in the present and being in the present means our complete agreement.

The heart is tickled seeing the pandal (marquee) covered with red and yellow clothes, the stage built at a height and the pillars of the stage laden with flowers. The flood of ambitions sitting inside wanted to come out and smile. The growing attraction of the public towards her was making her ambitions flourish, but the people around her wanted to destroy her ambitions by dividing them. They were hell-bent on dividing her voters on the basis of caste and religion and she was only looking at the voters.

"These are strangers; they belong to the opposition party. If you go, you'll have to drink water and tea from their house, we're their servants. We'll have neither religion nor money," a hardworking party worker had explained to her.

There were many other people with him. There was a whole group of men and women. Everyone was trying to convince her. These were the people who did not like her getting the MLA ticket, who had opposed her when she got the ticket. She had learnt to walk on the crooked steps of politics. She did listen to them, but did not argue. There was a crowd of people around her who were financially well off and understood that dividing the vote bank in the name of religion and caste was like shooting oneself in the foot.

"Nothing is more important than the party for me," she had given a straight answer.

"You have to bloom by living among thorns! There will be thorny bushes all around you. Your feet will be filled with thorns, but you have to walk unaffected, Amu. I have seen big politicians closely. It is my experience that when one progresses in politics, the difference between men and women vanishes. The person who knows how to navigate the sea of thorns will successfully cross it," Akash had explained to her.

It was a sea of thorns that Amrita had to traverse. She had to walk in the sea of thorns, even though her feet were already bleeding. She came out of Akash's arms and came to the open balcony. The wind had stopped; there was no bird on the cluster of trees. She was sweating profusely due to humidity. Black clouds were gathering, but it was not raining. Even in this heat, she was craving to smoke a cigarette. She lit a cigarette. As soon as the smoke of the cigarette came out of her lips, she felt a relief. The tension in both the jaws reduced. Relief was felt in the face, head and inside the body also.

One should know how to tolerate stress in life. We can do our work efficiently under the pressure of stress. She thought so, but she was shattered by stress. She wanted voters, not Hindus, Muslims, Christians or any particular caste. She had to win the battle. In the battle of politics, everyone is just a voter. These people were misleading her and taking her away from Muslim voters. They wanted to reduce her voters by spreading the fear of casteism. They wanted to defeat her and she ran from one end of every street of the city to the other.

She considered every house as her home. She had accepted everyone wholeheartedly and started loving everyone. Her love had expanded, in which the people of the entire city were in her embrace. Her consciousness was expanding where everyone was included. She had understood that for her high ambition, expansion of her consciousness was also necessary and all this kept happening on its own. She had crossed the limits; she had acquired the art of crossing the thorny ocean. The initiative of confession taught her to walk on the stairs and finally she won the election.

◇◇

As soon as she returned to the city and reached the bungalow, people started coming. Everyone was waiting for Amrita. It was the day when the official notification of her becoming a minister was to be released. There was no doubt in her mind.

At eleven in the morning she was officially

made the Home Minister of the state. For the first time in the history of the state, a woman was made the Home Minister of the state. Congratulatory messages were coming from the leaders of the opposition party as well. She was laden with garlands of flowers. Amit and Akash were standing together; there was happiness on the faces of both. Eyes were dazzling due to the glare of the cameras.

In response to the questions of the media people, she had to say every time that being a man or a woman did not matter in politics. Her responsibility was to be the Home Minister of the state, not to be a woman. She did not win the election even from the women's quota; it is the love of the people that has brought her there.

There was long coverage on TV of her becoming the Home Minister. Newspapers were full of congratulatory messages, but no one was reading them. Everyone wanted to register their presence in her heart and mind.

Crackers of happiness were bursting everywhere – at home, outside, in the city. People from every section of the city were participating in the procession. Prayers were being offered for her in temples, gurudwaras and mosques.

She was very happy. She had got a chance to do something for the society. It was a very good opportunity to do it by coming out of the narrowness of her personal life. Every fiber of her being was thrilled.

reading them. Everyone wanted to register

their presence in her heart and mind. Crackers of happiness were bursting everywhere - at home, outside, in the city. People from every section of the city were participating in the procession. Prayers were being offered for her in temples, gurudwaras and mosques. She was very happy. She had got a chance to do something for the society. It was a very good opportunity to do it by coming out of the narrowness of her personal life. Every fiber of her being was thrilled.

◇◇

"The more responsibility you take, the more powerful you become," Bauji had once said, and it was true. She had no complaints against anyone because she had to fulfil her responsibilities. She had to remain busy with her responsibilities. She also had no complaints against those who had many complaints against her and who did not want to do anything. They were scattered. With bags hanging from their shoulders, small newspapers in their hands and bearded, these were the people who were maligning her character. They were raising questions about her relationship with Akash, and unfairly pulling Amit into the discussion.

"Some such people are becoming very active in the city!" someone told her in the party meeting, but she had become deaf, dumb and had also put on the glasses of desires on her eyes. She knew that her reaction would fill the columns of newspapers. People smoking cigarettes at paan shops would say something about her that would make them all burst into vulgar laughter and one of them would double over coughing and hold his chest. She did not want to get bothered by these small matters, nor did she want to give people a chance to laugh.

Her silence made the atmosphere serious and discussions began on the safety of the people of the state. All this was expanding her thoughts, her feelings and her perspectives and this was also necessary for her to reach her goal. She could achieve something in politics only with her larger goal in mind. She wanted to achieve such a position in politics that would pave a path for the women to come without any conditions, where women could walk on their paths without any blemish and be highlighted towards humanity. While thinking, she felt lightness in her mind, as she was going to do a noble deed. The stream of people coming and going continued till late night.

“Madam ji, Amit sir and the kids are waiting for you at the dining table.” Amit and the kids must have called from inside.

She came to her room tired and exhausted. She went to the bathroom to get rid of the smell of sweat. When the fountain of cold water reached the top of her head, piercing her hair, she felt cool. Energy started flowing in the arteries of her body and she felt that flow of energy. She got into a happy mood and started humming.

"You look so cute in a pink gown, Mamma!" Tanvi’s compliment brought a shy smile to her

Amrita's face.

"Oh, I'm old now, daughter, you both dress up. You both enjoy your life. All the shopping shops in the city are open for you," saying this, she pulled Tanvi's cheeks. Amit and Tanvi started laughing, but Saanvi was turning the glass filled with water like a stone statue. She was ignoring her. Seeing this, Amrita was deeply hurt. She was broken from within by the opposition she had faced outside the house and only wanted love and respect from her children, but seeing Saanvi's body posture, her heart screamed with insult.

"Saanvi, look at Mummy, she looks so pretty and so young!" Tanvi had also started understanding now; she was going to college next year.

"Yes, if she is old, we might as well be young," saying this, Saanvi got up and left stamping her feet.

Amrita kept looking at Saanvi as she left, she couldn't even stop her. Her anger was at its peak. There was a sound of Saanvi's room door shutting with a thud. Tanvi too quietly left without eating. Amit was quietly drinking tomato soup with a smack, as if nothing had happened. She turned back to her room. She had taken off her pink gown. She wore a crumpled cotton saree from the clothes cupboard. She had made the drink herself and came to the balcony. She hadn't even put ice in the glass.

◇◇

She noticed a car or two passing by. A gentle breeze from the balcony played with her hair. The glow of the sodium bulb along the road offered no hint of moonlight, yet the moon shone brightly in the sky. The illumination cast on the pillars below did nothing to diminish the moon's youthful radiance.

"Hello, how are you?" The sound of Atiq's voice, so late, made her body tingle with excitement.

"I am fine," saying this; she adjusted the pallu of her saree as if Atiq was sitting right in front of her.

"Are you angry?" Atiq's voice seemed to be coming from a deep well.

"No, this is my fate. No one has a kind word for me, not even my own children."

She was crying and sobbing on the phone. She was in no mood to talk. After some time, she fell on the sofa in the balcony with the phone in her hand.

◇◇

"Mamma, wake up! It is seven in the morning. The drawing room inside and outside is full of people. Many people have come to meet you from outside as well. Papa is saying- Tell mummy to get ready soon."

She pulled Tanvi and hugged her. Tanvi snuggled into her.

“Tanu, you love me!” She was looking into Tanvi’s eyes. Tanvi tied her hair and started making a bun. Whenever Tanvi made a bun with her hands, she felt very relaxed. It was as if all the tiredness and stress of the whole day vanished away, the worries of the mind also reduced. Many times her mind became gloomy while meeting different types of people throughout the day, understanding their thoughts, knowing their problems.

“Mummy, you should rest for a while, you keep running around all day,” Tanvi was explaining to her. She wanted to tell her that she had grown up and become very wise. Now Amrita was not alone. The journey of her mind never made her feel that her children had grown up. Saanvi had said the truth as she had grown up. She would have to understand Saanvi too. She was on the threshold of youth where there was sentimentality, golden dreams and rebellious nature. She would have to face her rebellion.

"My daughter is very sensible," she thought, a smile spreading across her face.

Saanvi was standing hesitantly outside Amrita's room door.

"Come, my Rano. Come inside." She spread both her arms towards Saanvi.

"Mamma!" saying this Saanvi ran towards her and hugged her. Tears were flowing from Saanvi's eyes.

"Mummy, I'm sorry!" She saw that Saanvi's

eyes were wet with tears. Perhaps she too had not slept the whole night.

Amrita had drowned her sorrow in alcohol, but Saanvi, how much pain she must have felt the whole night. She knew that even if Saanvi had said something in anger, she loved her very much and rebellion also happens in love.

The phone was ringing. She picked up the phone. It was Atiq's call. She looked at Saanvi stealthily. Saanvi quietly left the room. Perhaps she had understood the importance of Atiq's call.

“Good morning! How are you?" Atiq's light-hearted voice brought her a sense of relief.

"I am fine. I want to meet you today!"

"Oh, you said what was on my mind! Today I’m also feeling like meeting you."

"Good!" She started looking for a nice saree from the wardrobe with the phone in her hand. Today she felt as if she did not have any beautiful saree. But it was also true that seeing her wardrobe full of many beautiful sarees, she started laughing at herself.

□

10

After becoming a minister, she realized that she had come even further away from relationships. There might have been no home, city, family or any other relationship; she had left. She was not so worried about her daughters now, but yes, she was cautious about them but that too was almost out of her mind. She was given a huge responsibility; the responsibility of the security of the entire state was on her. She was the Home Minister for herself, but for the political people around her, she was a woman. Everyone was eager to preach to her.

"I only became the Minister of Irrigation after thirty years of being in politics. I tried so hard to become the Home Minister, there was a demand of Rupees seventy crores (8.75 million USD), along with that some people were trying to get me a share, I did not like it. I was waiting for some people to come down, but you were made the Home Minister. Akash ji's money and influence worked because the Union Minister has a partnership in Akash ji's hotel business." Anoop Singh's eyes were making her feel dirtier than his words.

"That is not the case. Money is not always effective, so every party needs capable individuals who can make their party popular with the public. Yes, there is a real chance that people will embezzle money from those for whom ministerial positions serve only as a way to get richer. I'm sorry," Amrita said.

Anoop Singh's face clearly showed his displeasure at this, but the Home Minister was standing in front of him.

"Take advantage of my experience; you lack it." Amrita felt as though her body caught fire when Anoop Singh made this point very firmly. His eyes were getting red, and he had an alcoholic mouth odor. That person had a peculiarly negative effect; she became anxious and took a small step back.

“If you ever need me, please remember me,” Anoop Singh muttered and moved ahead.

As the State Minister for Irrigation, Anoop Singh was in a position of responsibility. Because of rape cases, he made headlines every day. He didn't feel guilty about saying offensive things about women. On TV, Anoop Singh was occasionally seen making offensive remarks about women. Since he was the actual brother of the national president of his caste-society, he took pride in his caste.

The politics of votes is also of a strange kind, where everything, legal and illegal, works. Just like for salvation, we have to come above our qualities-demerits, truth-falsehood and happiness-displeasure, etc. only then the path to salvation opens, similarly in politics also, one reaches power by crossing many moral-immoral, legal-illegal things and then expecting service to the public from such so-called 'honest' leaders is nothing more than a daydream. Although there are not many such leaders, but by using tricks they are able to enjoy the cream of powerful and lucrative positions; whereas honest leaders hesitate to go against their nature and keep watching with satisfaction. If they too put in their full strength, then the wrong leaders cannot succeed. Thinking this, she again got confused.

"I'll have to become a seer," a voice came from within. She did not want to react, she had forgotten this.

While going to the Legislative Assembly, many kinds of thoughts come to the mind like clouds. When the building that builds the society and the responsible people of the society sitting in it make noise by banging the table, then it seems that she has come to the colony of jackals and there is a crowd of jackals around her.

“Good morning, ma'am!" It was a greeting from Shalini, the lady MLA.

"Hello!" The sound of her voice triggered a memory of Shalini's tearful face. She often lamented that ‘people try to exploit the fact that I'm a woman.’ Her eyes would glisten with tears as she spoke, and she appeared weary, as if she were constantly being worn down."

"Look at you," Amrita said, her tone heavy with a dark satisfaction. "You're an MLA."

The reality of those words struck Shalini like a physical blow, and she wept, a raw, unrestrained sound of despair. She got the ticket due to the majority of a particular caste in a city of the state, the whole world knew that. Shalini was a sycophant of the society's president. It was heard that she had often been seen with Delhi's leaders in big hotels, that's why she became an MLA at a young age. She did not have the ability to work among the public, Amrita knew it, that's why she kept complaining. But if she said anything about her, it was said that 'a woman is the enemy of another woman'. She did not know whose conspiracy those lines were - she had not found those lines in any new or old book till date.

To get rid of her thoughts, she looked outside; the trees left behind on the road seemed to be laughing at her.

"But what kind of Home Minister am I, if even MLAs are not safe?" she thought, her expression growing tense.

She had reached the Vidhan Sabha Bhawan (The State's Legislative Assembly). The hall of the Vidhan Sabha was jam packed. Most of the people in the Vidhan Sabha were men, women were just a few in number. Everyone seemed to be excited about women safety in the state. As soon as she left, the opposition people started thumping the table loudly and there was a strange astringent smile on the faces of the party leaders. The

Speaker was reading something with his head bent.

"Three individuals assaulted a 10-year-old girl, who is now in the ICU of a government hospital. What action is our Home Minister taking?" asked opposition leader Agrawal passionately.

The opposition woman MLA crossed all limits; she screamed and said, "If it had happened to the Home Minister's own daughter, then she would have known how much crimes against women are increasing in the state." God knew what all she had memorized and written down and she was continuously speaking, while the Speaker was repeatedly asking her to sit down.

Amidst the noise of the opposition members thumping the table, she could not understand anything, all she could hear was - girl...women...rape...woman home minister...!

She closed her eyes, opened them when it came to a scuffle. There was a line of security personnel in the House. The Speaker had got up and left. She had to fight her own battle, no one was with her; not even Akash. She was alone, very alone. Her throat started drying up, her breath was going up and down and darkness started to cover her eyes. She could see both her daughters, frightened and scared. It seemed as if both the daughters were trapped among wolves; there was no open path in front of them. The wolves with sharp nails were moving towards them.

Suddenly she got up from her chair. “Calm down! Calm down! As long as I’m here, I won’t allow women and girls to be mistreated.” She had assumed the form of the goddess Chandi. Her shoulders had broadened, her waist had straightened and her neck had become taut. Her eyes had become fiery, seeing this everyone became silent.

“There is no need to exaggerate the matter of a ten-year-old girl and make a drama out of it. Everybody has a mother, daughters and sisters in their homes; it’s the joint responsibility of all of us. Though no one else may be held accountable, I willingly embrace the responsibility for the safety of the women in our state. How many of you stand with me?" Her voice resonated throughout the House. Silence spread in the House, only the soft sound of someone coughing could be heard occasionally.

She left the House like an arrow; Irrigation Minister Anoop Singh standing outside was staring at her like a wolf.

“Yuck, shameless!” she muttered and quickly left towards her car.

□

11

Even after holding meetings day and night, the problems were not ending, rather they were increasing.

“Ma'am, in Undri village of Sirpur district, the tribal community has set fire to the homes of the Rajputs. They have encircled Sirpur village, wandering through its streets armed only with makeshift weapons. A wave of chaos has swept over the entire area,” a voice reported urgently from the party office in Sirpur.

"What!" she said nervously. "But the police must be on-site, right?"

"Police are there but it is very far from the village; the police are afraid to come to the village. The villagers are climbing the hill and playing drums and shooting arrows at the police."

"Oh," she murmured, a hint of concern shimmering in her eyes.

"The police are helpless and the surprising thing is that the leaders of the opposition party are roaming in the village with the miscreants." On hearing this, she became alarmed.

"I'll take action right now," saying this, she disconnected the call.

◇◇

In a short while, Amrita was heading towards Sirpur with her entourage. The phone kept ringing.

"If you have any problem, tell me!" she was shouting on the mike, moving around the hill. No arrow came towards her, so the courage of the entourage was also increasing.

"Your problem is my problem, consider me your own and stop using the slingshot and come down. Talks are going on with the leaders of your community. I assure you that you will get justice," her voice was echoing. The leaders of the tribal area were with her, so her courage was increasing. Slowly, people were coming down the hill without slingshots, scared. She was assured seeing this.

The SP and his force standing in front were standing with their heads bowed. Many policemen were injured by the slingshots of the tribal people, but these policemen with her were also silent after drinking the bitter pill.

"Tents were set up for the protesting tribals on the plain below the hill." The tribals demanded a separate state and if they were to be fulfilled, it would mean to end their existence. The tribals were incited by the opposition party people by demanding a separate state. These innocent labourer tribals became victims of party politics.

There was a provision of food and water for the tribals. Everyone was hungry for many days. As soon as they were asked for food, they pounced upon it.

Amrita was busy talking to the officials in the tent when the tribals started singing traditional songs. After having food, everyone was dancing and doing Garba dance. Their anger had subsided, but Amrita's responsibility was increasing. She had to fulfil her promises, she had returned with this resolution. She had to make development plans in the tribal area with the help of local leaders. She stayed in Sirpur for three days with her entourage and returned only when the situation calmed down.

◇◇

Her trick worked, the whole area was happy with her wisdom, the only person unhappy was the irrigation minister Anup Singh. His trick failed. Amrita's wisdom was praised everywhere in the newspapers. Everyone was happy. Her stature was increasing day by day, people were conspiring to bring her down, but she was also ready to break their trap. She had acquired the necessary cleverness in everything from her clothes to her language.

Her photos in the village with a dupatta (Long scarf) on her head were printed in the newspapers, and her address to the tribals, 'Before being the Home Minister, I'm your sister, daughter and mother!' was made a headline in the media.

A sly smile was spreading on her face as she looked at various newspapers. Everyone was stunned that she had returned from Sirpur after setting everything right.

"You've done a great job!" said the president who had come from Delhi for the party office program, and every part of her body started throbbing.

"I've taken the problems as a challenge," Amrita said smilingly. Everyone had to clap.

"We face problems, but our problems also bring solutions, we've to find the solutions. Problems can never be bigger than us," she was saying this in her speech at the Government Girls College. The hall echoed with applause.

She wanted great newspaper coverage. As soon as Amrita looked towards the media, the shutters of the cameras started ringing and the videographers started shooting. She bent down and started talking to a very poor looking girl from the village, "What is your name? Which class do you study in?" She took out a bundle of ten rupees notes from her purse and handed it to her and kept looking at the cameras smilingly.

"Note down the name of this girl, she will get a scholarship for her studies from the Home Minister's fund," she told the PA (Personal

Assistant) and he immediately started noting it in the diary. She had very good relations with the print media and channel people, she used to generate a lot of news for them; and many times she had helped them in getting many benefits.

"Your political skills are increasing, which is a good thing but none of my work should stop. As long as you are the Home Minister, I'd definitely want to double my wealth. By now you must have realized that such powerful positions are not obtained in political career just like that, people remain ordinary MLAs and keep on folding hands in front of the secretariat officers but their pleas are not even heard and many poor people have to even sit on dharna (Protest)," Akash spoke, a mischievous smile and a playful twinkle in his eyes.

Amrita understood everything. He had become insecure due to her popularity and did not want to take any risk. She was getting out of his grip. Now she had started understanding the emotional exploitation of her people. Relationships were becoming a burden on her. She had signed right and wrong files worth crores (Billions) sent on the recommendations of Akash and this series was continuing. She knew Akash very well that in this world nobody helps anybody without any reason. People keep charging interest in instalments in return of a single help.

Akash's proximity was also beginning to bother her. As her external personality was expanding, she was shrinking in relationships. Her dual personality was getting a strong tether and she was flying in her dwarf sky.

She took a deep breath and tried to smile. That day she had shouted at Mahindra too, when he was repeatedly demanding to set up a factory.

"Bhaiya, now I've got to do something for everyone. I've a huge responsibility, and I've got to save my seat," she had spoken frankly to Mahindra for the first time. He had quietly left without saying anything. But she neither asked about his anger, nor called Bhabhi to inquire about Mahindra's well-being.

□

12

Amrita knew that politics is a tough job for the right people, but it is also true that if the right people stay away from it, the power will remain in the hands of the wrong people, which will make the lives of the people difficult. There was a crowd of negative leaders in front of her and because of them it was becoming very difficult for her to maintain law and order in the state. Her own people were creating trouble. There were heaps of cases of rape and harassment of women. Every morning the newspapers were filled with such cases, the court's stick was on the head of the police. It was as if they were sitting on a throne of thorns.

"Madam, this year we've witnessed a thirty-three percent rise in rape cases," stated the state's DG.

"Hundreds of cases are being registered every day. The list of cases is increasing due to the compensation amount given in rape cases." DG looked very worried.

"There's a session in the Vidhan Sabha next

week and I’ve to answer as a Home Minister.”

“The conviction rate in such cases is very low.” DG Sahab's voice also reflected concern.

“Most often in such cases, money is exchanged and the complainant turns hostile. The accused is released from jail,” the solicitor was also speaking with DG Sahab.

She was thinking about Ekta and her daughter. That morning, Ekta came with her daughter and was saying in a distraught tone, "Look! What Kamal has done to my daughter!" the mother cried, her voice breaking, as both she and her daughter sobbed.

“What happened to your daughter Ekta?” Amrita got suspicious. Ekta's daughter was crying with a handkerchief stuffed in her mouth and sobbing.

“Now how will we face the society? Everyone is already jealous of our family, everyone wants to humiliate us.” Ekta's brown eyes had turned red. She was crying with the pallu of her saree in her mouth.

"Now you call the police and file a report against Kamal." Ekta was telling Amrita authoritatively. Why wouldn't she? She was loyal to her. She used to give her all the news of the party, office, city and opposition. She used to go from village to village and contact people for her, before and after the elections. She was always ready for her.

"Earlier he used to say that he would marry me, he took me with him to hotels many times. Kamal had relations with me, now he says that he will have to marry wherever his parents say. He will get defamed in his society. His parents will never let him marry me because I am from a different caste," Ekta's daughter was telling Amrita while crying.

Amrita looked at Ekta's daughter carefully, she looked like an adult. She was probably around twenty five.

Amrita called the SP about this matter. Police action was taken in a hurry. The police had put Kamal in the police station. She had heaved a sigh of relief that day, but the very next day the media people had exposed the story of this rape. The front page was filled with big letters - 'The complainant retracted her statement after taking ten lakh rupees!'

Amrita held her head as soon as she read it. She was looking at the DG. She felt that he was also thinking something similar.

◇◇

"No, we'll have to be strict in such cases. Efforts will have to be made to strengthen the safety of women and police functioning will have to be improved," Amrita was addressing the journalists, but inside she felt as if she had lived for a few years. The darkness of the confusion spread about the identity of women was deepening all around, and she was drowning in the well of darkness.

She returned home with heavy steps. The entire veranda was full of people. Everyone had their own pain, perils and problems. She sat outside to listen to everyone. Listening to painful experiences reduces one's own pain.

Amrita took a long deep breath. She was really feeling relieved. She was recovering from her own problems, by listening to the problems of the people. Listening to the pain of others makes one's own pain less, the mind becomes light. It is said that we become closer to our soul in sorrow.

◇◇

It was nine in the morning. Amrita got ready and came and sat in the drawing room. This was a part of her daily routine. Sitting there she used to know the news from newspaper and TV and at this time Rasik Lal used to come almost every day with his bundle of information. It also contained a lot of useful information which the officers could not give. Then Amrita used to call the PA if necessary.

She saw in the newspaper that there was news in the headlines that ten prisoners had escaped from the Central Jail by jumping over the wall. In most of such cases she did not need to worry much because she had told the IG to call her only if it was very important otherwise everything has to be kept fine at his level.

Just then IG's call came, "Hello, what's the situation of the prisoners IG Sahab?"

"Don't worry ma'am, I'll make everything fine soon."

"Good!" saying this she disconnected the call and breathed a sigh of relief.

"How can ten prisoners escape together by jumping over a twenty feet high wall?" the reporters were asking. News was on TV. She was watching the news carefully while sipping her tea.

The police officer wanted to avoid the topic. "Investigation proceedings are going on, something can be said only after the investigation," the police officer was trying to avoid the questions by speaking rote words. Many times, police investigation means that everything is going to get messed up.

Just then Rasik Lal had arrived. He sat on a chair without saying a word and started watching the news carefully.

"How are you Rasik Lal ji? Have some tea," Amrita requested with a smile.

"Madam ji, when there is paan (Betel Quid) in the mouth, nothing else in the world tastes good at all, thank you." He was quite informal and treated Amrita like a family member. "What should I tell you Madam, when ACB (Anti Corruption Bureau) raided a constable, they found property worth crores of rupees and countless land documents, but to show the world, he kept on doing his duty on the roads in the sun on a police motorcycle," Rasik Lal had opened his bundle of information.

"This has become a common thing these days," she said smiling while sipping tea.

"Madam, some corrupt high officials had put him on this job. You won't believe that constable Shaligram has twenty bighas of land and four mines. He had also submitted documents for a petrol pump. The permission was just about to come when ACB caught him," saying this, Rasik Lal started coughing. His cough was not stopping even after drinking water. Maybe a paan was stuck in his throat.

"Did you get stuck with paan? Drink some water!" Amrita told him and he replied very innocently, "Madam, we get stuck with paan, swallowing it also creates problems, but these policemen should also get stuck with bribe sometimes," while saying this, he took out a handkerchief from his pocket and started wiping the tears coming due to getting stuck with paan.

"Let me tell you one thing, after a few days the jail report will come and one or two constables will be suspended, furthermore, the superintendent can also be transferred. The interesting thing is that the superintendent himself wants to get transferred, his wife is ill. He wants to go near his home. He will get posting near home due to this absconding case!" Rasik Lal was cursing the police administration again and again.

After retirement, Rasik Lal used to reveal all the secrets of his police department as if he had never been in this department, but the truth was what Rasik Lal was saying.

"These days, there's a rift between the administrative officers and the ACB police officers."

"Tell me clearly," Amrita said while placing the cup on the table.

"Madam, corruption takes place the most in the corruption department. Now who will control the corrupt people?

"Not everyone is the same, I believe so."

"I would like to tell you an incident from a few years back..."

"Wait, wait! I'll hear this incident later. I've to go now," Amrita said interrupting him.

It was as if Rasik Lal wanted to spill out everything today. There was a shadow of the past in his eyes, made up of many knots. It is said that until the tongue spills out what is in the mind, the mind does not get peace. The mind struggles like a fish lying on the sand at the sea shore and it shrinks. Shrinking of the mind is inviting sorrows; everything is insignificant in front of the mind. Rasik Lal also used to soothe the mind by putting it on the fountain.

The mind was getting restless seeing the shadows of the past and Rasik Lal was creating more doubts.

“According to your wish, you’ll stay here and I’ll remain in the same city as well. I'll let you know later," Rasik Lal said with a smile.

Amrita went inside to get ready and Rasik Lal went outside. In a short while Amrita left in her car towards an iron factory built outside a slum. Some labourers wanted to meet her there.

□

13

Amrita had reached the SP (Superintendent of Police) in a hurry. Such were the circumstances. In the remote hill village of Amarpura, a person had hanged himself at his in-laws' place. The same cast-people from many villages had surrounded that village. The administration had reached there with its staff.

"People, who do a job, do not put their lives at risk," a constable said and Amrita's blood boiled.

"Don't you have the manners to talk?"

He said staring at her, "Madam, you will leave after five years, we have to stay here. Secondly, I cannot use force on my brothers from our caste. It's a tradition of our society; it's been going on since the time of our forefathers," he said with folded hands.

This was being said by a man of law. Amrita was stunned. The law is nothing for them!

"Oh! Even copies of the Constitution have been burnt many times." Her body and mind started burning as she thought about it. How selfish we become when a wave of evil desires rises in our mind. In the alleys of dark roads, in the dark colony of lust, we even forget the fragility of life.

Her mind kept moving from clarity to confusion and from confusion to clarity, but she was unaware of being the doer and hence there was no inertia in her, due to which her creativity and progressiveness kept increasing. She wanted to go beyond all the problems, but this also did not mean that a policeman should speak illegal language.

"Tell me your name and belt number, Mr," she roared like a lioness.

Her secretary quickly opened the diary and took the pen in her hand. The policeman was staring at her, but she was standing firm with her convoy. Some more policemen had also come around her. Tension was spreading in the atmosphere with its secret conspiracy. Caste came first for everyone; country, society, humanity and nationalism were mere nonsense. The beds of their caste, spread for centuries, were spreading in their hearts and minds.

"You do politics in the name of our caste, you make schemes in the name of our caste, make the money and then Ignore us!" saying this soldier was getting angry and was screaming and telling about the pain of his caste.

"Government schools have been opened in

the villages, but where are the teachers to teach there? Those who are there do not teach, they make our children peel green gram. They make them bring the crops from the field. Have you ever listened to us?" his throat choked while saying this.

A policeman came running to Amrita and with folded hands said politely, "Madam, please do not feel bad about what he says. Ten bighas of his father's land has gone into the road. He has not received compensation for twenty years. His father has passed away. His young son is unemployed. He has not slept here for two days on duty that's why he is behaving like this." saying this, he started bowing his head.

The ambiance in that location was rather disquieting. The police were also becoming rowdy. Amrita turned towards the SP office. A crowd of rowdies from the nearby area was gathering there.

"I'll get it looked into right now," saying this, the SP Sahab called a meeting at the nearby police station. He himself went to inspect the spot. Local people had come from Amarpura and some people from here were also there. A few people were representatives of the house where the deceased had hanged himself.

"Sir, they're poor people," someone was saying.

"How much land do they have?" the moustache less Inspector started asking very authoritatively.

“The land must be ten to twelve bighas, Sahab,” the man said haltingly.

“Is it a well-irrigated or barren land?” A ray of hope arose in the eyes of the Inspector.

“Sir, it is well-irrigated and is adjacent to the highway,” another man spoke in between who was measuring the police officer with his eyes for a long time.

"Hey Hira Lal! How are you! Why are you standing there, come here," saying this police officer moved towards that man. Then both of them went a little distance and started whispering.

"Madam, let's solve the problem now. Please listen to this brother."

"How many bighas of land do you have?" Amrita asked that broker like person and he started whispering in her ear.

She smiled because she also needed land for brother's factory.

□

14

As Amrita's success and efficiency increased, so did the opposition she encountered. In politics, success and efficiency have different meanings. In politics, destroying people of your own party is success and walking with head held high in the shadow of lies is political efficiency; this is what she understood about politics.

"Madam, the hills have been cut around the city, many NGOs are protesting. There is uproar against our government everywhere!" when Dulhe Singh said this, everyone started looking at Amrita. The layout of the city nestled between the lush green hills and the water-filled lakes of the city attract tourists, and the Excise Commissioner of the entire state also sits here.

"You know, ma'am, people from outside come buzzing like flies here to build big hotels. They are investing a lot of wealth here. Almost all the ministers of the previous government have built hotels here. All the top police officials have settled here after retirement. They buy mines, invest money in hotels. The environment is already in danger," saying this, the district head of the rural area looked at Amrita. She knew everything. It is also a skill to pretend to be ignorant even after knowing, so she pretended to be ignorant.

"Make a list of such people; I want the names of their hotels and all the related information," saying this, she moved ahead, but there was a lot behind her that was making her restless – her opposition, the criticism against her, Akash and Amit, her increasing wealth, bank locker and accounts outside the country were on people's tongues. She had become a powerful leader, but was not powerful from within; she used to plead in private in front of the people around her.

"Is ACB taking any action against me?" she often expressed her nervousness in front of the IG, but his sly smile made her more scared. "Many bigwigs of the previous government have been in jails for the last three-four years. There may be all the facilities, but jail is jail," he was telling someone on the phone in front of her. The world is always looking for your weakness.

Amrita's growing ambitions had diminished her stature in front of her soul. Her consciousness was becoming narrow and her thinking was clouded; but ambitions were increasing. She wanted to take one or two more departments from the Chief Minister. She wanted to raise seven generations, but she was also surrounded by diseases.

"It's very important to control your blood

pressure and blood sugar, pay attention to your food and drink," the doctor would explain and she also understood. These days she would sit alone and drink till late at night. She had also distanced herself from Akash. Their relations were limited to their respective surroundings. Her two daughters were growing up and Akash had also expanded his business to foreign countries. Only formalities remained between them.

"Amrita, I still pray for you, I have no animosity towards you," Akash had said on the phone one day. When the income tax department raided Akash's house, Amrita's name was the first to come up. She had good relations with the income tax commissioner and in those days she had pressurized Akash to have Amit as a partner in Akash's hotel, but Akash flatly refused. He said, "Partnership with Amit will affect my status."

Amrita was looking at Akash in astonishment. Akash, who grew up in a very rich family, had a very good lifestyle, speech and expression, but it did not mean that he looked down upon Amit. A volcano had entered Amrita. She wanted to explode, but not by speaking, but by working skilfully. She met the commissioner herself, but later it was found out that a week after the raid, Akash and the commissioner were sitting together drinking alcohol. The Commissioner must have told Akash that she was losing even after winning every time.

◇◇

"You are being opposed, which means your strength is increasing. Do not worry," the former minister was explaining.

"I've come out of all the circumstances and am sitting in front of you. I spent six months in jail and saw the truth of the whole world."

On hearing this, Amrita's whole body shivered. Maybe he was scaring her or maybe she herself was scared of her deeds. Her heart always tormented her. Hundreds of workers were dying due to drinking alcohol. Forests were turning into fields. The money of government schemes used to reach the common people and it used to come in Amrita's account. Many lands in the city were in her name and she had partnerships in big hotels. From lime mines to marble, everything was in her name. People around her used to look at her with suspicious eyes and some journalists used to publish articles regularly to show her as a popular leader among the public.

While loading expensive sarees and jewellery, she often used to remember her mother who selected sarees and jewellery for every special occasion only on select occasions. Her mother's face shone with divinity. Her restrained life, restrained thoughts made her personality magnetic. She had nothing. No position, no status, no property, but still she looked like a queen. Her multifaceted personality was an example of her highest consciousness, while Amrita was roaming around with the burden of a dull consciousness like sometimes the fear of jail, sometimes the fear of police, sometimes the fear of court. She was sitting quietly like a fox, scared and frightened, sitting quietly in the shadow of trees in the dark, bowing her head in her own eyes.

The mobile phone rang. It was IG's call. Reluctantly she picked up the phone.

"Hello!"

"Madam ji, namaskar. Please give me some time tomorrow afternoon to meet, before you go out," IG Sahab was saying.

"Anything special?"

"No, I had to meet regarding the transfer of police officers," the I.G.'s voice was normal.

"Come anytime," she said, taking a sigh of relief.

Amrita's ambitions were staring at her and they started provoking her at the slightest opportunity. Transfer process of police officers is also a good opportunity to establish one's dominance. She threw her right hand in the air and closed her fist. Her driver, sitting far away, probably noticed her gesture. She started closing and opening her palms by throwing them in the air again and again, as if she was relieving the tension in her hands.

Today Amrita was at home. The drizzle of rain had refreshed her. Her cheerfulness was increasing in the pleasant weather. Calls were coming from the mines people continuously, she only had to sign. Her public number was set to divert calls to her PA. Today she wanted to relax. Just then her lawyer arrived without calling. Amrita did not like it, but now she will have to meet him.

“Ma’am, please sign the papers,” the lawyer wearing a black coat was saying.

“Here, at this place,” the lawyer said pointing his finger on the paper and she became alert.

MLA Deen Dayal had gone to jail in the case of signing the papers. He was able to come out of the jail only after several months. Her hand was getting weak while signing. She was repeatedly reading the paper by blinking her eyes. After signing, she was looking back. Who else could she trust more than her lawyer?

It was likely that the lawyer recognized her mood and said, "Please sign without any worry."

Her nervousness subsided a little with his assurance, but something was bothering her inside that how can she declare the mines as hers which are not hers, that too by signing the documents?

“I’m leaving,” the lawyer said keeping the documents in his briefcase.

“Yes, thank you,” Amrita could only say this much. Her head was getting heavy. She rested her head on the back of the chair.

She was unable to free herself from the fear in her mind. Sometimes she felt as if she had got a safe passage, which made her feel elated, sometimes she felt as if fear was penetrating deep into her mind, which made her feel dejected. She was unable to understand the games of the mind. From the outside, she appeared normal, but inside, her mind was overwhelmed with thoughts.

The pile of newspapers were lying there since morning, she did not get time to read the newspaper. She opened the newspaper and started reading but her mind was restless. She closed the newspaper and kept sitting staring at the ground. It was evening; the darkness of night was slowly descending on the ground.

All the good and bad things in politics happen at night only. Liquor mafia, land mafia; everyone comes to meet at night only. She was preparing herself to do everyone's risky work and charge a huge amount in return.

"The list of meetings is ready, ma'am," the PA was giving information.

"I'll be back just now, make everyone sit, let me have refreshments too," saying this Amrita went inside.

Saanvi was roaming around with a sulky face since morning. As soon as she saw her, she started shouting at the servants, "You people don't understand anything. You're taking a salary for free."

This act of Saanvi made Amrita think that she has become very cunning. Saanvi's fair complexion was shining even more in her long black open hair. Small diamond drops in her ears were adding to Saanvi's beauty, but her style seemed very absurd to her. She noticed that she had been looking lost for a few days.

"Mummy, Saanvi talks dirty to some boy on the phone," Tanvi told her mother the previous day.

“Oh!” Amrita suddenly blurted out, “I'll talk to her,” she was worried on hearing this.

“Saanvi, what's happening?” Amrita was furious at Saanvi.

“Don't explain to me how to talk to whom. I'm not talking like you. I know how you talk to that Atiq.”

Amrita's eyes went dark. Her own daughter was stripping her naked in front of everyone. She could not speak a single word. She saw that all the servants were avoiding her gaze. One by one, everyone started their work. She came to her room and collapsed on the bed, exhausted.

□

15

Amrita was getting ready; she had to go to the capital. The Chief Minister had called an emergency meeting.

"Madam, we must depart right away because we have a meeting at seven o'clock in the evening." The PA informed her.

"Yes, we're leaving now," saying this she started talking on the phone.

"Onions have never been this expensive! This is some conspiracy. They must have stocked onions," she started shouting on the phone.

"Elections are a year away, but the opposition is already playing political tricks," the senior party leader was saying.

"Yes, we also have to do something. I'm leaving for the capital now; I'll come and meet you, Namaste!" She hung up the phone.

Onions were missing from every city, village, and tehsil (sub-division) of the state. They had disappeared into thin air from the market, and no one knew what to do.

She started laughing even in such a difficult situation. Smiling even in difficult circumstances is an art. She remembered the story of Mulla Nasruddin in which his entire body was covered with bandages after getting injured, but Mulla Nasruddin smilingly says- "Everyone smile in equality, smiling in inequality is also an art."

Amrita burst out laughing, seeing this people sitting with her in the car also started laughing.

"Oh, the cunning people have made onions disappear! They have given a very bad blow. More than half of the people eat roti (flatbread) with onions only," When another senior leader who had accompanied her said this, everyone became serious.

This was also true. Onion was not only the pride of the kitchen of the poor, it was also an important part of the tasty food of big five star hotels.

When they got down at a hotel on the way to have lunch, there was a cross on the onion on the board outside the hotel.

"Oho!" Amrita said spontaneously.

Onions had been made to disappear from the market conspiratorially. All the businessmen had united against the government.

She was having her meal when a waiter came smiling with neatly chopped onions in a small plate, "Madam, this is all the onions I have in the hotel."

Don't know why, seeing the chopped onions, her hunger increased. The shortage of onions had increased her interest in onions. After having their meal, they went straight to the meeting.

There was a long debate in the meeting. There were plans on how onions would reach the public, but there were no onions. Anyway, Amrita returned after a four-hour meeting. It was a very serious problem. The opposition had attacked the hunger of the poor. Onion is the main food of the poor and it had been made to disappear from the market.

The next day, the public was on the streets against the government. Some young men and women were getting their photos clicked with onions in their ears and some around their necks like priceless expensive jewellery and posting them on social media. The entire social media was filled with photos of onions, onion jewellery and hue and cry about the shortage of onions. The opposition had got an issue, everywhere there was talk of onions only.

The intelligence system must be activated— where did the onions disappear? Everyone banged on their tables in agreement with the suggested solution when this issue was brought up in the following day's meeting.

The hall echoed with the slogan 'Inquilab Zindabad!'. Everyone saw a ray of light in the darkness.

The department had many conditions for the intelligence system to become active. All the conditions were accepted. The government seized the warehouses overnight. The logistics department became active. Piles of onions were piled up on the roads. All the onion mafias were hiding here and there. The opposition started talking about human rights but onions were again in full swing in the market. The failed efforts of the opposition brought the strength of the government to the lips of the people. The public was very happy, very relaxed. The public's faith in the government was once again strengthened. The opponents had themselves strengthened the government unknowingly.

Amrita now started preparing for the elections, but the problems were not going to end. The festivals of two communities fell on the same day. A meeting was held by calling the leaders of both the communities. Everyone agreed, but she was not convinced. She was repeatedly meeting the police and administrative officials.

"Madam, we'll try our best to ensure that there is no riot and the festival is celebrated peacefully," the police officer was reassuring Amrita. Her gaze fell on the wall behind his chair. Mahatma Gandhi's picture was neatly placed. The garland also looked fresh. It really seemed that arrangements for peaceful harmony had been made.

"Sir, the area from Gandhi Square to the left

to the Chudi Bazaar is very sensitive. Some mischievous people have set up camp there," when the smart and tidy police officer in uniform said this, deep lines of worry appeared on the forehead of I.G. He had got the posting with great difficulty and as soon as he arrived, this disaster had come.

"Deploy the force there. Bring the warrant from the court. Keep an eye on the people, especially those who are absconding and are now visible," as soon as I.G. said this, all the police officers saluted and left, but I.G. remained lost in thoughts.

That Sunday also came, when conches were blown on the open roads and naked swords were also used. People were pelting stones at each other. They were throwing turbans of some and caps of others. They sat hungry from morning to evening. Amrita also sat with the Collector, SP and other officials. Probably no one felt hungry that day. Everyone was passing the day by drinking tea only. This protest was to be called off only after a meeting with some special people in the evening. This was decided, but it was very difficult to control the unruly public till evening. If firecrackers were burst somewhere in between, everyone's heart would start pounding. If someone from the crowd screamed intentionally, the police personnel would get tensed.

Amrita felt as if everything would slip out of her hands, but she kept sitting patiently with courage and kept waiting for the meeting to be held that evening.

As the evening fell, the hustle and bustle increased. Unknown faces were also visible there.

“Probably these people will make some arrangements. These are the people who caused the ruckus,” Atiq was saying. He was regarded as a powerful leader with the support of thousands of voters.

“Okay.” She was looking at everyone fearfully.

“You should talk to Atiq ji, he is a good man,” when the police officer said this, Amrita became hesitant, but she also had to restore peace. Those who were trying to restore peace were shrugging their shoulders, so Amrita had to put her head on someone else’s shoulder.

She had met Atiq many times, but was not familiar with his influential personality. She was looking at Atiq with pitiful eyes. She could see a lot of votes in Atiq’s eyes and his eyes were reassuring her.

◇◇

"Don't worry, everything will work out." The carefreeness in Atiq's voice was evident.

She felt some relief. At least someone said that he could fix it. She was very impressed by Atiq. After that day, her meetings with Atiq started increasing. Atiq was really a good man. Amrita felt relieved seeing him, but Saanvi did not like her association with Atiq. Sometimes when Atiq came home, Saanvi looked very upset. Last time she had even humiliated Amrita in front of the servants.

"Mummy, I've told you time and again, I really don't like that man named Atiq coming to our house," Saanvi exclaimed, her voice rising with exasperation. "My friends won't stop teasing me about him, and they always have unkind things to say about you too. We have our own lives, you know!" With those words, she felt the weight of her emotions spill over, and tears streamed down her cheeks.

Amrita stood speechless. On one side there was political life and on the other side there was the satisfaction, self-respect and struggle of the children. She was standing far away and watching Saanvi hiccupping while leaning against the wall. Someone must have said this for Amit too. She has been informed many times that Amit is always going to the guest house with new women.

Amrita's heart became bitter. There is no question mark on the freedom of men in this society; the identity of women is made of holes of pain.

This Saanvi has also fallen prey to the same mentality, but Amrita was not going to back out now. She was fulfilling every need of her daughter, after that there is her own ambition and life.

Amrita turned and went to her room. Slowly the sound of Saanvi's sobs also stopped; perhaps she had gone to her room. Her mind was repeatedly telling her to go and sit near Saanvi, love her and remove her fear, but for some reason she did not go to her room.

□

16

"You'll have to decide whether you want a family or your career?" Atiq was telling Amrita. She had called Atiq in the morning itself and told him about the ruckus going on in the house.

"No, how can I neglect the family? There are young girls!" Amrita said and Atiq burst out laughing.

"Ah! You haven't even managed to keep them in line? If only you had, the young girls wouldn't be acting up like this." Atiq's voice had shifted, laced with a tone that cut deeper than any blade, yet she chose to swallow her pride and the sting of his words. She couldn't quite understand what had transpired with Atiq lately. Some days, he wouldn't answer her calls at all, and on others, he'd pick up just to cut the conversation short, claiming he was too busy. It felt as though everything had changed overnight, and she was left to grapple with the confusion.

"I'm leaving; feeling not well today," saying this, she got up and started leaving when Atiq's voice came from behind, "Khuda Hafiz!"

"Khuda Hafiz!" she said as she walked away. Today she was feeling distracted. Nothing felt good, even thinking about the voters and their problems. Perhaps she wanted a change in her life.

"Hello Kavita, let's go for dinner somewhere in the evening, we'll spend some time together, "Amrita called Kavita and she became happy. Kavita herself had booked a table in a good hotel and she came to pick her up on time.

"Today a very distinguished person has come to the city; I met him and told him about you too," Kavita was saying while driving.

"Leave this, friend, let your mind relax," Amrita said carefree.

After several days, Amrita noticed just how beautiful the city transformed in the evening. It felt as though life was dancing through the streets and plazas. The city, illuminated by vibrant lights, conveyed a multitude of emotions. Young couples were scattered everywhere, immersed in their own worlds. This is the time when we love someone without evaluating their traits, in a state of blissful ignorance. Once we gain insight, love often feels like a transaction.

"What're you thinking?" Kavita asked and Amrita came back to the present.

"Nothing, just like that; I was remembering the childhood days when we were carefree and loved our friends a lot. I can't do it now."

"You're not old yet, forty-four years is not

much," saying this, Kavita braked the car, the hotel had arrived.

In the hotel glittering with lights, the water splashing from the fountains was calming the mind.

"What did you think, Amrita?" Kavita asked while sipping whiskey.

"Nothing, right now the thoughts have made me restless, my mind is very restless. A decision taken with a disturbed mind can never be right. It's important for me to calm my mind, but how can I? I'm unable to understand this."

She was filled with restlessness. A sip of alcohol couldn't quiet her thoughts, so she pushed the glass away. Despite consulting a doctor that morning and receiving a clean bill of health, her mind remained troubled. The joy of her past had faded from memory, while the painful days of sorrow replayed relentlessly in her mind. Though she had once been respected, the sting of past insults, especially from those close to her, lingered in her thoughts. She longed to rise above the hurt, but her mind kept dragging her back into a cycle of painful reflections.

'Go to the hill ashram for a few days. It's a lovely and cozy place. Spend some time there and let everything else fade away.' Kavita was intoxicated, but her words echoed Amrita's thoughts.

"I was thinking something like this, Kavita," she supported Kavita and lifted her up. She had drunk too much, she was staggering.

Amrita had seen that hotel for the first time in her senses. All the men and women there were walking staggeringly. The eyelids of everyone's eyes had thickened. Everyone was drunk as if they were running away from stress. These people, who ignored the salute of the gatekeepers during the day, now look so troubled. They look so helpless under the influence of alcohol as if someone has squeezed the life out of their bodies. How the necks that used to be erect in the daylight have bent down helplessly! The mascara of the eyes of the women who used to look young by applying makeup was spreading below the eyes and ruining the well-made faces of those women. The pallu of the expensive sarees with diamonds and pearls seemed meaningless to Amrita. The ties that used to be erect around the necks of the men were hanging and mocking those rich men.

Amrita appeared to awaken after witnessing the scene before her. She resolved to visit the ashram that Kavita had mentioned to her. It was clear that she needed to make a change in her life.

◇◇

Amrita had set out in the morning to stay at the ashram perched on the hill. Upon seeing the serene entrance, she felt a wave of relief wash over her. Inside, the ashram was impeccably clean, and as she crossed the threshold, a sense of tranquillity enveloped her. The atmosphere, filled with the essence of verdant trees and flourishing plants, had an intoxicating quality. Once in her room, she opened the window and gazed outside. It felt like stepping into an entirely different realm. The men and women clad in white appeared almost otherworldly, each face adorned with a radiant glow and a freshness that was captivating.

"Knock, knock!" There was a knock on the door.

When Amrita opened the door, a beautiful woman was standing outside.

"I'm Ketaki, come with me in the morning yoga session," she said while introducing herself and a balloon of thousands of smiles burst from her mouth.

"Sure," Amrita said with a smile. She was giving her precious smile to her without any expectation of any benefit. Can politicians ever exchange smiles without any benefit?

"Yes," Amrita replied with a smile. She offered Ketki her cherished grin without any thought of personal gain. Can politicians truly appreciate smiles that come without strings attached?

"I'm leaving now. You should head to the dining hall, partake of something to eat, and get to bed early." With that, Ketaki turned and walked away.

◇◇

A week was nearly over, yet it felt as though she had been living in the ashram for years. Her days were filled with early morning awakenings, yoga and meditation sessions, evening satsang, and knowledge discussions. Amrita was enveloped in this new world, and her mind was slowly finding tranquillity.

The ashram buzzed with energy, hosting visitors from various countries attending the Gyan-Dhyan (Knowledge-Meditation) camp. From tall to short, dark to fair, and featuring diverse individuals like Jatayu (A man with a flowing beard and hair) and others who were bald, the space was alive with different people. In the dining hall, food was being prepared in large pots, while many gathered to chop a variety of vegetables, likely for lunch.

On that particular day, the ashram's refreshing atmosphere, shaded by lush green trees, felt especially delightful. The air was filled with the sweet fragrance of colourful flowers, including roses and jasmine, adorning the flower beds. Today, a gathering of saints was scheduled, and Amrita wandered through the ashram, her curiosity piqued, as this experience was unlike any she had known before. She felt a new lightness in her body and smoothness in her movements, as if her muscles had softened, and the weight that usually burdened her head had lifted. Her mind was clear, her body revitalized; she was encountering something profound and indescribable, a feeling that radiated through the smile blooming on her face.

“Today, great saints will visit for a knowledge discussion in the Yagnashala; you should sit in the front row,” Ketaki said as she approached. Amrita couldn't help but smile at the words. Ketaki was the only friend she had made on her first day, and her calm presence exuded a beauty that transcended the physical; it stemmed from the purity of her soul, illuminated by the surrounding atmosphere. Living in the ashram, Amrita’s perception shifted, leading her to see the inner beauty in everyone around her.

A sense of peace and joy grew brighter on her face as she began to recognize happiness in the trees, the birds, and even the sky above.

“Ketaki, you should come with me too," Amrita said.

"Of course, Didi! I'm coming along; I just want to grab some sandalwood for you," replied Ketaki as she moved ahead.

As Amrita walked through the ashram, she noticed many people around her. She didn't know any of them, nor did they seem interested in getting to know her, yet she felt a sense of connection with everyone. It was as if they all shared an understanding and a common purpose. Despite not recognizing anyone in the ashram, she did not feel alone.

Suddenly, a flock of birds flew overhead, chirping in unison. This sight filled her with excitement, and joy surged through her. She sensed her consciousness expanding, linking her to the essence of her existence.

"Didi, wait for me!" Ketaki called out, sprinting up behind her with a bowl of sandalwood in hand. Catching her breath, she smiled brightly, reminiscent of a child. That childlike spirit within us can surface at any moment. She applied sandalwood to Amrita's forehead, and within moments, Amrita felt a soothing sensation throughout her body, her mind opening up.

The air in the Yagnashala was rich with the scents of incense, kewda (Screw pine flower), and blooming flowers. A gentle fragrance enveloped Amrita, making her feel as if she were soaring through the sky. Although her feet remained planted on the ground, but her spirit danced above the clouds.

Outside the Yagnashala, there was a long line of people waiting for permission to enter. Amrita, noticing the crowd, ignored them and approached the entrance. Just as she thought she could walk right in, a man by the entrance instructed her to join the queue.

"You've violated the rules; you'll need to go back and wait in line," he said. At that moment, it felt as though a hundred droplets of cold water had been poured over her.

As the Home Minister, Amrita was accustomed to being addressed with respect and courtesy. Anger flushed her face. She glared at the man, but he remained focused on checking the documents of the others, completely unaware of her presence. Turning around, she discovered that Ketaki was no longer beside her; she had likely fallen behind. A sense of humiliation washed over her as she felt everyone's eyes upon her. Her dignity was bruised. After a brief internal reflection, she realized that it wasn't dignity she felt wounded, but her ego. She had crossed the fine line between self-respect and ego by standing there.

Amrita turned her head to survey the crowd once more, but no one was looking her way; everyone was absorbed in their own lives. Convinced that she was indeed invisible to them, she stepped back and took her place in the scorching sun. Yet the heat didn't seem to unsettle her. Instead, she felt a growing desire to understand herself in this new environment. Her past life, filled with mundane activities and chasing fleeting pleasures, had not brought the fulfilment she now experienced in this moment. The warmth of the sun seemed to penetrate her very soul, providing a sense of joy she had never known.

When Amrita finally entered the Yagnashala, the chanting of mantras had already begun. A saint sat on a high seat with his eyes closed. She felt a strange familiarity with him, as though she had seen him before. Despite having merely glimpsed him, she felt a profound connection. The atmosphere settled into silence after the Yagna-havan, enveloping everyone in a serene calm.

◇◇

It had been nearly a week, and Amrita's thoughts began to take on a new shape. She felt a strange inner conflict between her old and new ideas, as if she were navigating a period of transition. Ultimately, she arrived at a peaceful realization: while politics was her passion, it shouldn't consume her to the point of making life burdensome. She recognized that what she had experienced in her brief life was enough, and gratitude filled her heart. Now, she needed to balance her household responsibilities with a serene approach to her work, ensuring that both her career and her family were infused with joy.

□

17

As Amrita returned, she felt a surge of freshness upon entering the city for the first time. A sense of relaxation enveloped her, coupled with a desire to embark on new experiences, albeit in a different manner. She no longer wished to be swept along by the currents of life; she possessed all the essentials—respect, wealth, and accomplishments. Yet, she found herself adrift, plagued by negativity and sorrow, lacking a path to connect with God and transcend duality.

Amrita yearned for the spiritual journey from duality to non-duality, seeking to encounter her beloved Lord, gain self-knowledge, and cultivate introspection. Her journey had transformed into one of withdrawal, as she sought balance by turning her unruly five senses inward.

Having grown weary of sensory pleasures, she now desired to stop wandering. Her goal was to connect with the supreme power, and this longing alone shifted her perspective on life. She aspired to initiate her new Karma Yoga by forging a connection with her soul, no longer willing to endure a one-sided, incomplete, and unconscious existence.

She hadn't been able to see Saanvi since she got back. Maybe Saanvi was avoiding her because she was upset. Amrita thought about how people frequently inadvertently become isolated from their loved ones when they achieve greater success. She reflected that failure, not success, is what truly causes loss.

Rising from her seat, Amrita filled a glass of water and drank it quickly. As her mind settled, thoughts of Saanvi resurfaced. She dashed out of her room, determined to climb to the upper floor.

“Mama, be careful on the stairs! You might fall!” Saanvi exclaimed as she spotted Amrita hurriedly ascending and rushed to meet her.

“Saanvi!” Amrita's voice trembled with emotion as she enveloped Saanvi in a warm embrace, as if to never let her go again. In that moment, she held the childlike version of Saanvi close. Saanvi sobbed, while Amrita's eyes overflowed with tears of pure joy, her smile beaming. For a few priceless moments, she held Saanvi in her arms as she revelled in the overwhelming joy of reconnecting.

“Mummy, can we go shopping today?” Tanvi joined them, wrapping her arms around both of them. Amit stood nearby, watching the scene unfold. Their eyes met, and a smile spread across his face for the first time in years. Amrita noticed the streaks of gray in his hair and the deepening circles under his eyes; his gaze carried the weight of too many nights spent drinking, his health deteriorating as a result. For the first time in many years, Amrita felt something stir within her for Amit.

“Amit, come on! Let’s all play together in a circle,” she suggested, eliciting surprise from her daughters as they noticed the change in her demeanour.

Suddenly, a playful smile ignited on Amit's lips, sparking laughter that filled the room. After all this time, they were smiling together as a family, the sound of their joy filling the air.

“Amit, I’ll be busy in a meeting today, so please take care of the children,” Amrita said as she began to descend the stairs, her daughters calling out, “Bye, Mama!”

She halted abruptly, glancing back at Saanvi, whose dimples deepened with her infectious laughter. It had been so long since she had seen such a pure smile.

"Bye sweetheart!" Amrita said to Saanvi, and she started waving goodbye with a smile and laughter.

Hurrying down the stairs, Amrita checked the clock–it was half past ten. She needed to leave everything else behind and get going. Once in the car, she reviewed her meeting notes. The agenda was the same: fuel prices, road construction, inflation, women’s safety, and child welfare, among others. However, the statistics showed no improvements, even as the government's accomplishments were the talk of the town.

Upon arriving at the venue, Amrita found it packed to capacity. Today's meeting was with journalists, media, and administrative officials, who were bound to ask the same questions she had addressed the day before. The media's cameras were focused solely on her, while the officials sat attentively in their chairs, creating an atmosphere of composed professionalism.

After a two-hour meeting, she exited the hall feeling a deep sadness. She had so much to offer society, but not under these circumstances. She was tired of living in the illusion created by government statistics. Her eyebrows knitted together in frustration, prompting the PA standing before her to step back in trepidation. Dressed in a platinum ring and gold watch, he was making plans for the disadvantaged!

"Mr. you need to better yourself; I won't allow corruption to persist any longer," she said, her eyes fixed on the gleaming gold watch.

"Yes, ma'am," the PA replied, his confidence diminished. He quietly retreated from the scene.

As Amrita ignored the approaching collector, he turned to look back at her. She stood tall, like a warrior, having emerged from the meeting with a renewed sense of purpose. She had spent her whole life working hard to earn a name and wealth. Now, she only wanted to work like a karma yogi, where selfless service would be the only purpose.

After she completed the Aarti (worship), she would ask her father what service meant, and he would respond, "Service is a work done without any expectation of reward."

"I must serve now, without wanting anything in return," she muttered to herself.

◇◇

When she returned home late that night, fatigued yet sober, she felt no urge to drink. A profound sense of peace washed over her, filling her with a different kind of satisfaction. She recognized that having positive thoughts and performing good deeds nurtured her mental tranquillity, while negativity stirred restlessness and a desire for alcohol. True humanity, she believed, lay in empathizing with the struggles of others, and Amrita aspired to reach a consciousness that allowed her to grasp the pain of those around her. She could mitigate their suffering—after all; God had endowed her with the capability. Tears filled her eyes, and she felt overwhelming gratitude towards the divine presence that governs all. Her hands joined together and rose upward in prayer.

The night deepened as she settled down to sleep, but suddenly she sensed a presence nearby. When she opened her eyes, she saw Saanvi standing before her, eyes cast downward.

"Can I sleep next to you?" Saanvi asked softly, and Amrita welcomed her with open arms, pulling her close.

◇◇

The next morning, as they gathered around the breakfast table, Amrita reflected on how she had learned that material wealth alone does not bring fulfilment; true satisfaction is found in emotional connections. She began to experience the joy of contentment with her family and was motivated to reconsider her approach to work. She realized she needed to commit not just to herself but also to her community and family. While commitment can be challenging, its long-term impact is always rewarding.

She sensed that Saanvi was drawing closer to her like a trusting child. The resentment that once lingered in Amrita's heart was dissipating, bringing a newfound calm toward her daughter. Yet, Saanvi seemed withdrawn, almost fading away. Tanvi mentioned that Saanvi no longer spent late nights on her phone or going out; she was focused on her studies instead.

It was 9 PM when Amrita sat in her room, engrossed in a book about selfless Karmyoga, when she heard footsteps approaching her door. In moments of tranquillity, even the faintest sounds become perceptible. She looked up to see Saanvi entering, looking lost and sorrowful.

She approached her mother and sat with

her head bowed. Amrita gently lifted her chin, and Saanvi rested her head on Amrita's shoulder and began to cry. Something had clearly broken within her—perhaps Saanvi's spirit. Amrita instinctively began to soothe her back. She had learned at the ashram that comforting a sad person by lightly stroking their back could offer solace. The touch of her hand began to bring relief, and gradually Saanvi's expression shifted from despair to calmness, her hiccups diminishing.

"What's wrong, Saanvi?" Amrita asked in bewilderment.

"Nothing, Mom," Saanvi mumbled, her eyes averted. The redness from crying stained her face, and her lips looked dry. During moments of sorrow, a person often reflects closely upon themselves, and in that stillness, Saanvi's true beauty began to emerge.

"Please, share your troubles with me," Amrita urged, holding Saanvi's face gently between her hands. A small smile broke through Saanvi's sombreness at this familiar gesture.

"Really, Mom; it's nothing," Saanvi replied, attempting to pull away.

"You must tell me everything, dear." Amrita's seriousness returned, her eyes locked onto Saanvi's.

"I ended my friendship with Harshad. He isn't a good person; I'm sorry," Saanvi confessed, her gaze cast downwards.

Amrita regarded her in silence for a moment, her suspicions confirmed. She understood that parents must navigate such situations with patience and care.

“It’s not important, just forget about it,” Amrita said with a serious tone.

“But Mom, he has my photos. I gave him all the money he demanded and I didn’t tell you, but he’s still holding onto my pictures. He’s asking for more money, threatening to go public with them, and he keeps insisting that I meet him again and again.”

“How dare he!” Amrita’s body shook with rage, and her eyes seemed to spark with fury.

“Harshad says terrible things about you too, Mom. Please, I need your help!” Saanvi exclaimed, wrapping her arms around her mother.

Amrita pulled her aside, her fingers swiftly dialling a number. Her voice was calm yet firm as she said, "You don’t have to worry anymore. He won’t even dare to whisper your name—not even in his dreams."

A sense of relief washed over Saanvi's face.

□

18

Amrita has been having a great time exploring the rural areas. Upon arriving in the villages, she is greeted by everyone as though she were a member of their family. She had decided to forgo lavish decorations and expensive tents for her election campaigns, opting instead to embrace a simpler lifestyle, akin to that of the villagers.

Witnessing women break stones by the roadside deeply moved her. The radiant beauty of a woman glistening with sweat made city beauty salons seem insignificant, but the haunting hunger of these women under the blazing sun remained an unaddressed issue.

"How many children do you have?" Amrita inquired of a young woman draped in a yellow shawl, who was part of a group of labourers.

"Four children, madam," the woman replied hesitantly, adjusting her shawl over her face.

Amrita was taken aback; the woman appeared to be no older than twenty-five.

“Four children!” Amrita’s jaw dropped, eliciting laughter from the other women.

“If a girl marries at thirteen, she becomes a mother while still quite young. Just four days ago, six girls were married on Akha Teej (A festival),” explained a woman adorned with a gold nose ring set with red and green gems. In Rajasthan, villagers often tweak their dialects to make them sound more like Hindi for better understanding.

“Married at thirteen!” Amrita was astonished. She couldn’t fathom that such practices still occurred today, especially when the administration was present in the villages during Akha Teej festival.

She looked around and shouted to her party members, "This is illegal!" There was a faint smile on everyone's faces.

“If we grease the palm of the police chief, a younger girl can be married off alongside an older one, allowing us to settle them both in one go. If there are three girls, we can settle them all at once,” Ganga Ram, donning a white turban, remarked, while nearby policemen glanced awkwardly and the Tehsildar (A Sub division administrative officer) walked off with his file.

Amrita pondered how to promote girl education in the villages. When she visited local girls’ schools, she found dilapidated buildings gathering dust. In some schools, female teachers were seen knitting sweaters or making students shell peas, while in others, the poor students sat idly waiting as their teacher napped.

"No, this cannot continue; we need concrete action!" She resolved to make regular visits to the villages and called her PA to instruct the Collector, SDM, and Education Department officials to issue letters from there.

A sense of determination blossomed in Amrita's mind as she travelled to neighbouring villages. The issues mirrored one another: child marriage, dowry, women travelling long distances for water, dry taps in homes, and a lack of tolerance toward young girls.

She felt overwhelmed by the sight and stories she encountered. Frustration bubbled within her as she scolded herself for the negligence of those in authority.

◇◇

Amrita returned from her rural tour. Today, a meeting was scheduled with police officers, administrative officials, local leaders, and women's organizations. When the Superintendent of Police arrived, he immediately sat next to Amrita without greeting her and pulled out his phone to start a conversation.

Unable to hold back, Amrita interjected, "We're in a meeting, and it's about to start."

"Oh, this isn't my first meeting with you. I've attended many before," the SP replied insolently. The SP continued, brazenly addressing the women in the front row, “It’s nice to see such beautiful women.”

“Enough!” Amrita shouted.

Startled, the SP exited the meeting abruptly, caught on camera by reporters. The attendees were left stunned by the incident.

Debate erupted during the meeting, with each participant expressing their views. Everyone was grappling with insecurity and a desire for self-protection. The atmosphere became creatively charged, and the media praised the meeting despite the negative behaviour of the SP By the following day, the SP had received an Awaiting Posting Order (APO). Amrita felt unburdened by any fear of the police. Her focus was now solely on public welfare, leaving no room for apprehension. Fear only thrives in greed, desire, and attachment. As she grasped the fleeting nature of life, she found herself becoming more detached and fearless.

Her relentless dedication and wise decisions were creating a stir in the political landscape. The public began to appreciate her more, boosting her confidence and fostering unity among the people. She empathized with the suffering of others and shared in their joy. However, as her popularity grew, so did opposition from political adversaries. In party meetings, discussions arose surrounding her drinking and smoking habits, her close relationship with Akash, and the legal troubles concerning her mining operations. Efforts to undermine her credibility on moral grounds were intensifying.

Omkar Singh was anxiously pacing back and forth during those days; he was actually the mastermind behind the opposition group. In fact, he wanted to keep Amrita out of politics at any cost. While he had secured his ticket for another term, it was now unmistakably clear that Amrita was destined to become the Chief Minister. The high command had already made an announcement, stating that only Amrita could manage the party's ongoing factionalism and thwart the opposition's plans. It was common knowledge that her fighting spirit had earned her the nickname "Shaktimaan" (Super human being), while her empathy had drawn her closer to the public.

That day, as she was leaving the Vidhan Sabha (The State Legislative Assembly), she unexpectedly encountered the minister known for his inappropriate behaviour, a womanizer. A wave of anger washed over Amrita. She still recalled that day vividly.

"Hello, ma'am," he said, standing before her with hands clasped.

Amrita turned her gaze away.

"Ma'am, the ACB (Anti Corruption Bureau) is after me and insists on arresting me. Please help me," he begged.

A sly smile crept onto Amrita's face as she replied, "Of course."

"It's SP Goyal from the ACB," the minister said, filled with hope.

"Alright, I'll speak to him!" With that, she got into her car, leaving him standing outside with his hands still clasped in desperation.

Once inside the car, Amrita called Goyal Sahab, "Hello!"

She laughed on the phone with him, and Goyal Sahab chuckled in return.

"I'll take care of it right now. I won't let him reach home, I promise, ma'am."

Amrita felt a wave of relief wash over her as she listened to Goyal Sahab's reassuring words. The weight that had burdened her for years was finally lifted, allowing her mind to feel lighter. Shortly after, the minister was arrested and taken away in a police vehicle, while the media swarmed around him. The city's atmosphere had shifted dramatically, and once again, the streets echoed with praises for Amrita

◇◇

Amrita's workload increased as the elections drew near. To stay energized, she practiced yoga and pranayam, which provided her with a refreshing sense of vitality. This practice did not drain her; instead, it filled her with energy. Her thoughts were becoming broader, and her efforts were expanding. All her negative habits faded away, making those with a negative mindset around her feel uncomfortable—resulting in her embracing a more positive outlook.

For Amrita, the realm of politics resembled Kurukshetra, with the public being her most powerful weapon. She dedicated every moment to securing her victory, breathing life into her mission. Her guiding principle was 'Soham', meaning 'You are, so I am.' A subtle current of energy, like a gentle breeze, often enveloped her, sparking a vibrant thrill within her very being. As her Sattva deepened, her work became a seamless dance, reshaping both her inner self and the world around her.

◇◇

On that day, Amrita was taken aback to see Akash in front of her. He had changed significantly.

When Akash greeted her with a cheerful "Hello!", Amrita returned the smile with warmth. It had been years since they last met.

“Hi! How have you been?” she asked, and Akash couldn’t help but return her smile.

They sat together for a while, and it was clear that Akash was pleased to see Amrita’s election preparations. They chatted about various topics before he folded his hands and took his leave, wishing her well. The encounter felt healthy and respectful. Neither of them dwelled on the past. Embracing the present is the key to a fulfilling life. Living in the moment offers an attraction to life, while clinging to the past only brings sorrow, as the mind tends to focus on negativity. Meanwhile, thoughts of the future are often fraught with uncertainty and doubt. The present is a vibrant space filled with creativity and vitality.

After meeting Akash, Amrita felt her mind lighten, bringing her joy. She cherished this positive interaction, clear of any negativity. Satisfied, she shifted her attention to the colourful hibiscus flowers flourishing in the pots.

□

19

The entire city was abuzz with election chatter. Opposition parties were making concerted efforts to rally together, while certain members of Amrita's party were conspiring internally to undermine her efforts. Omkar Singh was openly cautioning Amrita, and lately, his interactions with opposition members had noticeably increased. New illegal liquor stores had begun to crop up across the city, encroachments on government property were on the rise, and the administration showed no signs of curbing these intrusions. Leaders had emerged on every street corner, with released criminals asserting control and some even attempting to stand for election themselves.

"Ma'am, Suresh Bakri wishes to see you," the PA said, a hint of shyness in his tone.

"The same Suresh Bakri whose brother was killed in a police encounter in Madhya Pradesh related to an MLA's murder?" Amrita queried, recalling the details.

"Yes, Ma'am," the PA replied, now more at ease.

"Alright, ask him to come by tomorrow," she said, and then continued her phone conversation. During election season, it was essential to engage with everyone; this was part and parcel of public relations.

At that time, violence such as stabbings and shootings had sadly become commonplace in the city. The atmosphere of fear during elections had become a ritual. While there used to be moments of tension in her mind, Amrita had learned to manage it, which she considered an achievement.

“Just yesterday, there were shootings on the main road in the morning and stabbings in the evening. The culprits, the police, and the witnesses —everything stays unchanged," she mused.

Someone had even informed her over the phone that Omkar Singh was frequently seen carrying a pistol with a group, fostering fear among the residents.

Suddenly, Amrita's car came to a halt in the face of an obstructing crowd. People began shouting slogans against her and the government. While the anger was palpable, she could tell that these individuals were not from her city; she recognized the locals even by their shadows.

There were around twenty armed individuals, and the shop shutters along the road were pulled down. Passers-by hurriedly retreated, while the crowd mockingly laughed in front of her vehicle. The driver was silent and visibly anxious, yet her bodyguard remained alert.

Chhuttan Bhaiya, seated in the front, was visibly tense, though he tried to maintain composure, swallowing hard at intervals. This was all happening in broad daylight, in her city.

Although she faced armed crowds, she remained calm at heart. In that moment, she took a breath, opened the car door, and stepped out to confront them.

"What do you want?" she asked, directing her gaze at a figure whose face was obscured by a black cloth, leaving only his eyes visible.

She exhibited no fear of death, a fact that unsettled those around her. The crowd started to disperse as they saw her brave attitude. Amrita understood that their intent was merely to intimidate her, but she met their gaze without flinching. With courage, she felt enveloped in a protective aura; true security comes from faith, not from possessions or people. In that moment, she surrendered her fears to the Almighty.

.The hired thugs lacked the nerve to meet Amrita's eyes and gradually fell back. She returned to her car with steady footsteps. During this period, Amrita was cultivating a unique sharpness of mind and an inner richness. She was no longer troubled by trivial matters. Her commitment to daily yoga and deep meditation had imbued her with profound self-assurance. With a pure and sattvik diet (Pure and wholesome food), her thoughts too were becoming sattvik, leaving her with a sense of lightness in both mind and body.

Amit had undergone significant changes lately, almost as if he had withdrawn into solitude. There were no more late-night parties or any of his previous bad habits. He had given up alcohol due to liver damage, and as a result, he had become more serene and content. Most of his time was spent at home or in the company of Amrita. Sometimes he enjoyed light music, while at other times he delved into books by emerging authors. He also managed his business online from home. Their bond had deepened into a harmonious connection, embodying true togetherness. They had truly become ideal householders, and family life felt like a shared journey of devotion. Now, their family had expanded; everyone was part of their extended family.

◇◇

In the soft light of the morning, Amrita sat quietly at her desk in the office when Bakri entered the room.

He greeted her with a respectful bow, "Namaste, ma'am."

Amrita acknowledged him with a nod.

"I just wanted to let you know," he continued earnestly, "if you have any tasks for me, please don't hesitate to ask. I've even turned down requests from other parties for work."

Curious, Amrita inquired, "What kind of work are they asking for?"

“Madam, if there's any challenging task that needs to be tackled, please don’t hesitate to let me know. I'm willing to take on even the toughest of consequences, even if it means spending a few days in jail.

Her expression darkened as she replied, “You would actually accept such a task? Don’t you feel any shame at the thought of going to jail?”

Unfazed, he retorted, “Ma’am, even big leaders have faced jail time. We’ve seen that before.”

His audacity was evident, and Amrita recognized the implications of his words. She knew such individuals thrived on chaos, and in the sensitive climate of election season, crossing them could spell disaster.

“How many of your associates are in jail?” she probed, a spark of intrigue in her voice.

Bakri's eyes grew wide with astonishment.

“Get your people to apply for parole; during elections, they just need to hold peaceful rallies!” she suggested.

Comprehending her point, he nodded attentively, prepared to depart.

She firmly added, "And keep in mind that your job is to bring everyone together and cooperate, not to incite riots."

He stood speechless for a moment, as if wrestling with newfound embarrassment. “Yes, ma’am, I’ll take care of it,” he finally managed, bowing his head as he exited.

However, the political landscape was murky; others in a clandestine party meeting voiced concerns about purchasing the votes of MLAs, emphasizing the need to carefully calculate their strategy. Amrita, determined to maintain her integrity, had to negotiate the appointments with the higher command, ensuring that the right candidates received their due positions.

This secret gathering stretched over three days, taking place in a hidden venue filled with the scent of kebabs and the clinking of glasses. Yet Amrita chose solitude, retreating to her room each night to eat simply. Omkar Singh, left behind in the political fray, showed increasingly shady intentions. After consulting with the higher command, she made the tough decision to revoke Omkar's ticket, introducing a fresh-faced student leader in his place. This shift transformed the energy within her party, as the new leader brought enthusiasm, intelligence, and a refreshing perspective steeped in spirituality.

At last, the chaotic rush of elections subsided as the code of conduct took effect, and everyone eagerly anticipated the results.

Finally, the long-awaited day arrived, and Amrita's office buzzed with candidates, all focused on the television.

Her party had secured a decisive majority, a victory that was not just hers but shared with many. Cheers erupted; chants of "Bharat Mata Ki

Jai!" filled the air, creating an electric atmosphere of celebration.

As the clock struck six, the city sparkled under a canopy of red and yellow lights, balloons danced in the air, and rangoli adorned every home. Streets overflowed with joyful dancers, lifting Amrita on their shoulders in a moment of triumph. Camera flashes illuminated her face amidst the frenzy. Yet, even in the midst of joyous chaos, she remained grounded, her inner calm unwavering. She understood that nothing was everlasting, recognizing the importance of dedicated service with a sense of detachment—considering all worldly successes as mere illusions.

◇◇

Amrita sat quietly beneath the colourful pandal (Marquee), the vibrant celebration swirling around her like a whirlwind. Laughter and shouts of joy echoed through the air, the microphone amplifying the exuberance of those celebrating her. Yet, amidst the revelry, her mind drifted into silence. Her eyelids grew heavy, prompting her to surrender to the darkness behind them. A wave of helplessness washed over her, as if she were adrift in a sea of indifference, detached from the festivities and its fervour.

From the distance, a voice floated through the air, weaving its way into her consciousness.

"Vaishnav Jan To Tene Kahiye Je Peer

Parayi Jane Re."

(That person is a true devotee/righteous person who understands the pain of others.)

In that moment, Amrita felt a deep yearning within her soul to embrace the melody emanating from 'Vaikhari - The Divine Voice'. She longed to connect with the haunting strains of the song. With a gentle nudge, she delved deeper into her being, her spirit exploring uncharted depths. 'Vaikhari - The Divine Voice' song transformed, resonating within her heart, igniting a thrill that surged through every fiber of her being. Tears began to flow freely, like a joyful tide cascading from the depths of her inner ocean, sweeping away the weight of her worries. Her eyes remained closed, but an innocent smile crept upon her lips, a testament to the joy blossoming from within. In that sacred stillness, she gleaned an insight: politics had become an empty vessel, stripped of the divine essence that spirituality brought.

The world echoed with chaos, a by-product of this detachment from spiritual guidance. Amrita sensed a calling—a need for transformation in the world of politics, to weave spirituality into its very fabric. This, she realized, was an urgent necessity, a beacon of hope in turbulent times.

•••••

अधूरी कहानियाँ
रागिनी प्रसाद
धूप की लकीरें
रागिनी प्रसाद
रागिनी प्रसाद
वैखरी
रागिनी प्रसाद
शाकम्भरी
रागिनी प्रसाद
To buy visit
www.newlifemedia.co.in

www.ingramcontent.com/pod-product-compliance
Ingram Content Group UK Ltd.
Pitfield, Milton Keynes, MK11 3LW, UK
UKHW041356190726
13845UKWH00041B/550

9 788198 586223